Diary N Death
Harbor Inn, Maine
by Teresa Ives Lilly

Published by
Lovely Christian Romance Press
Copyright 2017 All Rights Reserved

DIARY N DEATH

CHAPTER ONE

"Wait right here, Bill. I won't be long." Sylvia May spoke in short, clipped words as she unfolded herself from the taxi's back seat and swiped down her mid-calf length gray skirt.

"But Miss Sylvia, you know I might have a call come in, and I can't wait too long." He spoke in a pleasant Southern drawl, which always turned people's heads, since he lived in Maine.

Sylvia cocked her head sideways, her short-cropped silver hair remaining in place, then allowed a small smile to twitch across her face. Her eyes sparkled with mischievous laughter.

"Bill, you know everyone in town is here today. No one will be calling for a ride. Look around." She slowly moved her arm in a semi-circle indicating the street and driveway jam packed with cars.

Bill, a fortyish, balding man with a gentle smile and piercing blue eyes, pressed his lips together. He knew there was no point in arguing with the older woman. After all, he was the one who always told his friends on the Wednesday night bowling league, "When a woman turns seventy, you just have to give the lady her way." And Miss Sylvia was seventy-two.

"I'll have to keep the meter running." His voice sounded stern, but Sylvia noted his hand reaching across the front seat and pushing the meter lever to off, not that it mattered as they had a special deal worked out.

"You are a dear. I was just writing in my diary this morning about our unique relationship."

"Relationship!" Bill's eyes bulged with surprise. "I'd say it's more of a dictatorship. You give the commands, and I do the driving."

Sylvia turned and gazed at the Mansion. This was one home in Maine she loved. It was considered one of the finest Italian

Villa style homes in America. Built by the Pendecot family in 1858 near the city's earliest gas and sewer lines, it boasted hot and cold running water, flushing toilets, central heating, gas lights, a servant call-bell system and wall to wall carpeting from day one. Over the last century and a half, the family changed the home very little, with the exception of modernizing only the essentials.

Sylvia noted the crowd near the front door of the old mansion beginning to move. She patted the large book bag hanging off her shoulder, which was currently empty.

"I promise not to be long," she called back after turning and beginning to scuttle to join the crowd.

Bill sat back with a deep sigh. He knew what "not too long" meant when Miss Sylvia was on the hunt at an auction or estate sale for a handwritten diary.

There was no doubt, in a place as large

as the Pendecot mansion, Miss Sylvia would be scouring every room for books and diaries to add to the unique collection she kept on hand at Good Old Days Antiques, which was nestled in the Harbor Inn Courtyard. She would be no less than one hour.

"Don't know what that woman sees in diaries written by other people, but she sure goes wild for them."

Bill relaxed and closed his eyes. His bark was worse than his bite. He had a soft spot for Miss Sylvia and wasn't about to go off on another call when she might need him.

"Morning, Miss Sylvia," a heavy-set man in his late forties called out as Sylvia entered the mansion. Hubert Acorn was the Estate Sale Guru in Harbor Inn, Maine. He'd been raised in the business and took over after his father passed on. He had a boyish smile and friendly way about him, but Sylvia was aware that he knew the value of every item in the homes where he ran the estate sales. There was no haggling with him.

"Good morning, Hubert. Did you locate anything I would be interested in?" She eyed him carefully.

Hubert stepped closer and pulled her away from the front door so she wouldn't block the way. "Not this time, I'm sorry to say. It seems the whole lot of Pendecots didn't believe in keeping track of their daily lives. I searched the bookshelves but found no diary."

A bit of the sparkle left her eyes. "Hmff. Well, I suppose there are other items I can purchase for my shop. Especially since next month is the Coast Drive Mile Long Yard Sale. I want to be well stocked. Those crazy people, who come from all over the United States, will buy almost anything."

Hubert chuckled. "Well, it's your turn to get the leftovers from this estate sale. I gave the last bunch to Hatty. There wasn't much in that sale so she wanted me to give her the leftovers from this sale as well, but I told her it was your turn."

Sylvia reached over and patted his hand. "Bless you, Hubert. I appreciate you dividing up the leftovers from estate sales to the different antique dealers in town. You could just donate them all to the Senior Thrift Store. However, I better stay out of Hatty's way for a while. If she's upset, I'm sure I'll suffer, one way or another."

"I'll have Jennifer log everything that's left over, box it up and have it delivered to your shop. Probably be two weeks. Of course, you can't expect any jewels; the famous Pendecot jewels were lost."

Sylvia cocked her head, "Hmm, jewels. I think I remember hearing about jewels."

"Well, it seems there weren't any jewels anywhere in the house; at least none have been found. They would be part of the estate, though, which would be quite a chunk of money."

"Who gets the money?" Sylvia asked inquisitively.

"I'm not sure. They read the will a month ago, but family members have been pretty tight lipped. I was called in to do the estate sale." Hubert explained.

Sylvia nodded in understanding. Families were usually the problem when it came to these things.

Hubert continued. "The lawyer, Drake Johnson, is in charge of getting the final check from me. He'll be the one to tell me whom to make the check payable to."

Sylvia smiled. Just then Hubert called out, "Jennifer, go help Mrs. Blackston. She's trying to reach something on a shelf that's too high for her."

Miss Sylvia noted the girl behind the counter, smiling at a young man who was slung across a chair nearby. The girl jumped up and rushed across the room, just in time to catch a vase, which a woman almost toppled off the shelf.

"It must be nice to have your daughter here on summer vacation working for you."

"It is, but it's not just vacation. She's finished with college now. Trying to decide if she wants to come into the business or not. It would be great, except that Jason Jones is hanging around her." His brow furrowed.

"Jason seems like a nice young man." Sylvia tried to smooth his ruffled feathers.

"I don't trust him. He has a record, didn't you know?"

"A juvenile record for breaking and entering the high school several years ago. He was with a group of boys who thought it would be funny to put peanut butter on the principal's chair. I wouldn't call that a real record. He does work for many people in town now. He just needs a good steady job. I wouldn't worry about Jason and Jennifer."

Hubert didn't look convinced but shrugged and turned when he noticed someone waving for his attention. He excused himself.

Sylvia turned and faced the open floor plan and scanned the rooms. The gorgeous woodwork throughout the house pulled her attention. The spiral staircase seemed to call to her, but bedrooms usually held the least interesting things, so she decided to start on the downstairs floor.

Not the kitchen, or living room. What she needed was a library.

Hmm, since there is no diary to worry about, I think I better start with the bookshelves. Never know when I might find a first edition.

Sylvia May took three steps in the direction of the library where she could see shelves loaded with books, but before she could go further, she noticed Hatty standing across the room, arms akimbo, staring at her. Sylvia took another step toward the library but Hatty moved quickly, pounded into the room and began pulling one book off the shelf at a time; flipping open to the first page.

There's no point in looking at the books. Hatty is sure to make it unpleasant. I'll leave those first editions to her this time. Sylvia turned, feeling irritated. She didn't want to be in competition with Hatty, but ever since Hatty opened her Blue Willow Antiques across the square from Sylvia's Good Old Days Antiques, Hatty'd considered herself in competition with Sylvia.

Well, the one thing I know Hatty won't fight me for is larger pieces of furniture. Her shop is too small to hold them. Sylvia noted a large desk, shoved against the far wall. For now, she would start there, and work her way in any direction Hatty didn't go in.

Sylvia pushed her way through the crowd, but she made a beeline for the desk. There were several large boxes sitting on top of the desk. She looked around, hoping to see Hubert, but decided he must be in another room, so she carefully lifted one of the boxes off the desk and set it on the floor here it could easily be found. She was surprised that the box was empty. The other few boxes were also empty.

It's as if someone placed them here on purpose, to cover the desk.

Her eyes scanned the room again. No one seemed interested in what she was doing. If someone was trying to save this desk for themselves, they weren't in the mansion now.

Sylvia stepped back to take in the whole desk. Although it needed a bit of work, she was amazed at its beauty. It was a Queen Anne Style Burr Walnut Leather Top Desk, probably from the 1920s. It was a pedestal desk with fine carvings all over. The top boasted three tooled leather inserts. The graduated drawers were serpentine shaped with the original brass handles and locks. The feet were carved from solid walnut.

Sylvia moved closer and slipped open the top drawer. There were several pens and a stack of paper in the drawer. She pulled out each drawer but found nothing else. Finally, she pulled out the front drawer, bent down and basically crawled under the desk hoping to find a date or inscription hidden under the drawer, but to her surprise, wedged at the far back, behind the drawer in an obviously added on secret compartment, was a black leather book. More than likely a ledger of household accounts.

Sylvia pulled the book from its hiding place, stood and stepped toward the window to get better lighting. Without her magnifying glasses, she could no longer read fine print, but in good lighting she could easily get by with most print.

When she opened the book to the first page, a rush of excitement shot through her. This was not a ledger.

The first page read, "The personal diary of Mrs. Mary Pendecot...."

Sylvia put the diary back into its hiding place and turned slowly around to see if anyone was watching her. When she saw Gathe Denver across the room, she held up a hand and waved. He was one of her favorite antique dealers. He always found good deals and passed them on to her. He'd recently married a girl from Texas named Tricia. It was a bit strange to see him here. He and Hubert were not on very good terms. They were both vying for the same estate sales in town.

Just then Sylvia saw Hubert again and waved him over. She pointed at the desk. "Hubert, I think I'd like this desk."

Hubert's eyes opened wide in shock. It wasn't like Sylvia to purchase such a large item. She usually chose books, knickknacks, and small end tables.

"It's mighty big for your shop."

"A bit, but I think I can turn it quickly. Besides it has some unique features I'm especially interested in." She cocked her head and winked at him.

The man stared at her as if she were crazy. "Got something in your eye?"

Her shoulders shrugged.

Hubert was a nice guy, a shrewd businessman, but a little dense around the edges.

"No, I'll just take the desk. I'd like to pay for it now, before anyone else gets interested in it. There were some boxes sitting on it, as if someone had already laid claim."

Hubert shook his head. "No one mentioned a desk. But I think it's the same one that was in that article last week."

"What article?"

"The Harbor Inn Gazette ran an article about lost jewels and missing coins from the Pendecot estate. No one knows exactly where they are, but that desk was in the main photograph of the article."

"Hmm, I'll have to get a copy. That's probably why the desk wasn't in a specific room, just pushed against the wall."

Hubert wrote out a ticket and told her to take it up to the front door.

Before she reached the front, a tall, thin woman with greying hair approached. She wore a beige pencil skirt and pleated white button shirt.

"So, you've found my grandmother's desk?" She looked directly at Sylvia, but her lips formed a thin line. There was nothing pleasant in her question.

"Oh, is it? Wasn't it for sale? Hubert told me I could buy it."

"Unfortunately, it was for sale, and Hubert just informed me you were purchasing it."

Sylvia felt a wave of dismay. If she wasn't able to purchase the desk, how would she get the diary.

"So, is it for sale or not?"

"Yes. I would love to purchase it, but I couldn't get the funds, no matter what."

Sylvia was taken aback. "But...but if you are the granddaughter... there should have been..."

"Indeed. There should've been plenty of money left to me. But my grandmother didn't leave any money to and one in her family. There were some jewels I'd hoped she would leave to me. She knew how I loved them... But, she left the entire estate to charity."

Sylvia felt awkward, it was obvious the woman was bitter about this. "I'm very sorry, but I heard the jewels were lost."

"I'd hoped to find a clue to where my grandmother hid them..." The woman's voice faded away. "My grandmother used to write in an old book."

Sylvia swallowed. She should tell this woman about the diary in the desk, perhaps it belonged to her, but something held her tongue.

The woman stared at the desk and seemed to be mesmerized as she spoke. "I can remember as clearly as if it were yesterday, watching my grandmother sitting at that desk, writing..." her voice faded and her eyes met Sylvia's.

Sylvia stood silent, wondering what to do or say. Estate sales were awkward enough, but to actually have to purchase items while family members were standing by was completely uncomfortable.

The women stepped to the desk and began pulling open the drawers. Sylvia watched her open each one and then slide it closed. Sylvia fidgeted with her purse, hoping the woman didn't find the diary.

When the woman had opened and closed all of the drawers, she straightened, her face pale and even grimmer looking.

Sylvia put out her hand. "I'm Sylvia May, by the way. And you are?"

"Alice Pendecot." The woman did not return Sylvia's handshake.

"Do you live in the area?" Sylvia asked, edging her way to the front counter.

"No. I wasn't able to get here until yesterday. I missed the reading of the will, but that doesn't matter since no one in the family gets anything. After the estate sale, I'll be heading home."

"Where is home?"

"Georgia."

Sylvia smiled; she had noted the southern drawl in the woman's voice. "It was nice to meet you."

The woman just turned and walked away.

That was strange. However, I can understand her attitude if she wanted to own this lovely desk. But it seemed like she was looking for something.

Sylvia frowned. By the way Alice was searching the drawers, she wondered if the woman knew about the diary. Sylvia wanted to look around the sale a bit more, but the idea of leaving the diary behind worried her. Alice might come back once Sylvia was gone and find the book. Sylvia got down on her knees, crawled under the desk and plucked the diary out of its hiding place again. She slipped it into the bag on her shoulder; then she stood and looked around the room. Several people might've seen her, but Jason Jones was definitely staring at her. He leaned over and whispered something to Jennifer.

"Sooo, I found a few surprises on the book shelves," Hatty's voice caused Sylvia to jump slightly. "There was even a first edition."

Sylvia shrugged. She wanted to moan when Hatty told her the title of the book. She would love to have the book, but she wouldn't have missed out on the diary, even for a first edition.

"I'm glad you found a great deal." Sylvia stepped aside and began to head toward the front again. Hatty noticed the ticket in her hand.

"What are you purchasing, Sylvia?"

Sylvia sighed and pointed at the desk. Hatty's eyes grew large, and Sylvia was sure they turned green with envy.

"That desk. But, well, you don't usually purchase..."

"No, usually I look at books first." Sylvia almost laughed when Hatty covered her mouth with her hand in surprise.

Maybe that will teach her not to shop the books first in the future.

"There's been some talk about this desk," Hatty stated.

"Really?" Sylvia asked.

"Yes, several stories going around. Something about jewels and coins."

"I hadn't heard anything."

Hatty stepped closer and reached out as if to open a drawer. Sylvia cleared her throat.

"I'm purchasing the desk, Hatty."

Hatty pulled her hand back as if she'd been burned. Her eyes squinted at Sylvia. "Did I see you slip something into your bag?"

Sylvia shook her head and walked away. She didn't want to outright lie, but she wasn't going to tell Hatty about the diary in her purse.

Sylvia wandered through the rest of the house. She picked up a few trinkets then set them down, but nothing major caught her attention.

When she stopped in the dining room, she was mesmerized by the wall made of small square mirrors. Each mirror was rimmed in gold. She reached out to take one from the wall, to check the price, but was surprised it didn't budge.

"Won't come off the wall. They were cemented on." A tall, dark haired man spoke from behind her. Sylvia jumped slightly and turned to face him.

"I'm Peter Pendecot." He stuck out a

hand and gave Sylvia a strong shake. "I'm the grandson."

"Oh, are you Alice's brother?"

His face seemed to cringe. "Nope. My mom and her dad are brother and sister. We are cousins, but we never met before today. She spent a few summers here; I came for Christmas."

Sylvia was intrigued. Perhaps the diary would give more insight into the reason why the grandchildren visited at different times of the year.

"I'm sorry about your grandmother's death."

The man shrugged. "She was ninety-five. Couldn't live forever. I wasn't close to her. Just so you know my true character, though, I came here just to hear the reading of the will. I hoped I would get something, a small fortune or just a few thousand, but no doing. The old lady left it all to charity."

Sylvia frowned. She did feel sorry for the

two grandchildren. It didn't seem right that their grandmother left them nothing.

"Used to be some old coins around. My grandfather owned them. I was quite attached to them. Used to stare at them for hours. I'd hoped she would give them to me."

"Oh, I heard they were lost."

"Seems that way. No one has found them yet. But even if they did, it's all part of the estate. I couldn't afford to buy them."

Hubert happened to be walking past and called into the room. "Sylvia, I think there are some teacups you might like in the dining room."

Sylvia nodded and looked back at the mirrored wall. "It's truly exceptional." She assured Peter, however, as she glanced at the wall, something didn't seem right. She tried to decide what but couldn't quite make it out. She finally moved on to the dining room and kitchen.

Just then, Sylvia heard the loud voice of another person she knew. Doc Holiday had just entered the front door. The man was the epitome of an old cowboy. He wore the twenty-year-old cowboy hat, faded and overused jeans, and a too big for his body belt buckle. To top it all off, there was always a wad of chewing tobacco in the side of his mouth.

Why his parents chose to name him Doc Holiday, no one knew; their last name was Digby. But that was the name he'd been given. He was a coin collector.

"Heard there was a mighty fine old desk for sale today, Hubert." Doc's voice rang across the room.

Sylvia moaned.

Hubert shook his head slowly. "Was one, but it's been claimed."

"Claimed? Claimed? What does that mean? If it's not been bought, then it's still for sale. I'll take it." The man reached into his back pocket, pulled out a long wallet and started pulling hundred-dollar bills from it.

Hubert's eyes searched the room frantically, then landed on Sylvia. She nodded and moved toward the front door.

Sylvia reached the front desk and handed her ticket to Hubert. Gathe Denver was leaning against the counter.

Gathe looked at the ticket. "I see you're purchasing Mrs. Pendecot's desk. It's a real beauty. A bit masculine for a woman, but sturdy. I had my eye on it myself. Thought I'd like it as an office desk, unfortunately I didn't have a chance to look it over."

Sylvia was a bit taken aback at his tone. She'd always known him to be so pleasant, but something in his voice made her feel she had displeased him.

"When you have time to stop by, I'd love to have you look it over with me. Help me decide on a price." Sylvia smiled as she reached into her bag for her credit card.

"I thought about buying it for myself. I

saw it in the Gazette last week. It reminded me of something my grandfather used to have in his office. I wanted to show it to Tricia, but she couldn't get here until later in the day."

"Well, bring Tricia to my shop to see it."

Gathe smiled with a nod.

Just then, Doc Holiday's voice interrupted them. "I've got good old American cash here, and I want that desk." He almost pushed Sylvia out of the way.

Hubert frowned.

"I'm sorry, Mr. Holiday. I claimed the desk first. I don't think cash or credit make a difference in the purchase." She looked toward Hubert who nodded in agreement.

"What you want an old clunker like that for?" The man's voice rose in irritation.

"As an investment." She bristled slightly. "I need not explain myself to you." She turned and pushed the credit card into Hubert's hand, and he began to slide it through the credit card reader.

"Now just you wait," The old man tried to grab the credit card from Hubert's hand.

"No, I don't have to wait. I have the rights to make this purchase.

"That's correct, Miss Sylvia. Now Doc, stop causing trouble." He turned back to Sylvia. "And you want it delivered to the shop?"

Sylvia bobbed her head.

Hubert wrote something on her ticket. The transaction was completed fairly quickly.

"We'll deliver it to your shop on Monday morning. Don't worry about meeting me there; I know where you keep the key."

Hubert handed her the receipt. Sylvia picked up her bag and made her way to the front door. She wasn't able to purchase anything else; but the atmosphere was so hostile, she felt she should leave.

Before she stepped outside, she turned

and looked back. Alice Pendecot, Hatty, Doc Holiday, Gathe Denver, Jason Jones and Jennifer were all staring at her. Not one friendly smile could be found.

Sylvia shivered then walked out the door.

Goodness, estate sales are getting more cut-throat each day. All that hostility over a desk. Perhaps I shouldn't have bought it after all. I could have just asked Hubert to sell me the diary. But, the desk is so unique. Yes, a bit pricy, but I love it. And finding a diary hidden inside makes it so much more valuable.

Before she reached the waiting taxi, she stopped, turned, and slipped back into the mansion. No one was at the front desk now except for Jennifer.

Sylvia glanced across the room and saw another man looking at the desk. He seemed to be a casual shopper and didn't open any drawers. Unlike the dark haired Pendecot grandchildren, he was a rather short man with blonde hair.

"I've decided to have the desk I just bought delivered to my house, instead of the shop. I'd like to keep it for my own personal use. Can you work that out?"

Jennifer nodded, pulled out the sales ticket and made a note on it.

"We do our shop deliveries on Mondays so it will arrive at your house on Tuesday," Jennifer explained.

"That's fine. In the meantime, could you please strap it closed? I don't want everyone pulling the drawers out."

Jennifer nodded. Just then Jason came up to the front. Jennifer pulled out some long, mover's straps and asked him to help her wrap up the desk.

"Do you know who that man looking at my desk is?"

Jennifer looked up then shook her head. "Never seen him before."

Sylvia finally made her way out the door and toward the taxi. Bill was leaning against the front panel, a toothpick hanging from his mouth.

"So, did you buy anything? Your bag looks kind of empty."

"Yes, I got a lovely desk, and I did find one special treasure." She patted her bag.

"A diary?"

Sylvia held a finger to her lips. "Shhh."

Bill nodded, opened the door and waited until Sylvia slipped into the seat. As he walked around the car to get in the driver's side, he laughed.

She always finds a diary.

CHAPTER TWO

"Where to?" Bill asked when Sylvia was settled into the back seat of the taxi. "Back to the Good Old Days?"

Sylvia laughed. How she would love to go back to the good old days! But now the only "good old days" for her was the antique store she owned.

"I'd like to stop at the Harbor Inn Nursing Home. I haven't seen Laura Lee in a week."

Bill nodded. Laura Lee was Sylvia's older sister. The two women lived together until a year ago, when Laura Lee fell and broke her hip. After that, she wasn't able to care for herself, and Sylvia couldn't do it either. That's when they decided Laura Lee should move into the nursing home.

"How's she doing?" Bill asked as he pulled away from the mansion.

"Fair to middlin'. But she's quiet these days. The doctors think she's showing signs the first signs of Alzheimer's."

Bill looked into the rearview mirror and noted Sylvia wipe her eyes with a small hankie. In his sympathetic voice he said, "Now, I'm right sorry about that, Miss Sylvia."

Sylvia waved the hanky at him. "It's to be expected. She was already frail. Remember, she is eighty years old."

Bill nodded and drove on. Sylvia told him about finding the diary along the way. When he pulled into the circular driveway in front of the nursing home, Sylvia glanced up and said, "Now Bill, I don't know why I feel this way, but please don't mention to anyone that I found a diary in the desk I bought."

Bill swished his hand back and forth across his chest. "I promise. You know you can always count on me, Miss Sylvia."

She patted her hair into place. "I know, and usually it wouldn't make any difference, but for some strange reason I thought Alice Pendecot seemed a bit too interested in what might be in the desk. She did mention a diary, but until I get to read and document it, I don't want anyone to know about it. However, once I've finished, I'll ask Alice if she would like to see it."

Bill rubbed his fingers across his lips like a zipper being closed. "Your secret's safe with me."

"There did seem to be a lot of interest in the desk itself. I thought I was going to have to call the police."

Bill frowned. "Why?"

"That old coot Doc Holiday was trying to get the desk."

"Hmm, wonder what he wants it for? He usually goes for the coins."

Sylvia tilted her head. "That is exactly what I'm wondering. I can't wait to have a good look at the desk. Maybe there's a hidden compartment I didn't see."

"What if there are some old coins worth a fortune?" Bill laughed.

"I'll let Doc have them."

Bill nodded. He was sure that's just what Sylvia would do. She'd never consider herself first.

He stopped the car by the front door, turned off the engine and got out. He moved around to the other side and opened the door for Miss Sylvia.

"Can you wait for me?"

"Sure can. I'm off the clock now so you have me for the rest of the day."

Sylvia smiled and walked to the front door of the nursing home and went inside.

Bill watched her go in then leaned against the taxi. Because she didn't drive, Miss Sylvia used the taxi service so often, the company no longer charged her by the mile. They just charged her a monthly fee. Bill often drove her around after he was off the clock. She was sort of the grandmother he never had. And since his wife passed away and his kids were all grown and living out of town, there wasn't anything else for him to do most of the time.

Just then, a rather rough looking man pulled up in an old Ford truck behind the taxi. He beeped his horn several times so Bill got in and pulled the taxi to the parking lot. He sat in the car and watched as the man left his truck in front of the nursing home and stomped inside.

Sylvia found her sister sitting in the dining room at a small table with one other woman. They were early but anxiously waiting for their lunch.

"Hello, Laura Lee." Sylvia leaned over and gave her sister a hug.

Laura Lee stared at Sylvia for a moment then suddenly said, "Oh, Sylvia May, it's you."

"Yes, dear." Sylvia sat in the chair beside her sister.

"Where have you been today, Sylvia?" Laura Lee asked.

"I went to an estate sale at…"

Suddenly, a man stomped up to the table. "Mother, I went to your room, but you weren't there!" His voice boomed causing Sylvia, Laura Lee and the other woman at the table all to jump.

"I'm sorry, Donald. It's almost lunch time." The woman sounded nervous.

The man pulled a chair up beside his mother. "It doesn't matter. How are you?"

Sylvia realized she'd been holding her breath. The man must not be as bad as he seemed because the other woman was smiling and talking in an animated way.

She turned back to her sister and continued her conversation.

"I went to an estate sale at the Pendecot Mansion."

"Oh, I was sorry to hear that Mary passed away."

"Yes, I was as well. But I bought a lovely old desk, and guess what was hidden in it?"

Laura Lee shrugged, "What?"

"A diary. I'm sure it's Mary Pendecot's own personal diary."

Laura Lee's eyes lit up. "That's wonderful; she was a rich woman."

"Yes, but her granddaughter told me Mary gave all her money away to different charities and organizations. She did say there were jewels hidden somewhere, but no one has found them."

Laura Lee nodded. "I remember those emeralds she wore at the Mayor's Ball several years ago."

"Yes, and the rubies she wore to church. But they're gone now, or hidden." Just then, the attendant set a tray of food down for Laura Lee and the other woman.

Sylvia squinted at it and gulped. It didn't look very good, but Laura Lee assured her the food here was wonderful.

"There was an article about the jewels in the Gazette last week. I haven't read it yet. I think it talked about some missing coins, too."

Laura Lee cocked her head and in a rather loud voice exclaimed, "Missing jewels and coins! That sounds interesting. I'd like to read that Gazette article, too."

"Shh!" Sylvia's eyes scanned the room. The man sitting with his mother was staring openly at her.

"I don't know anything about the jewels and coins. As I said, I found a diary inside the desk I bought."

"Maybe she wrote about them in the diary," Laura Lee whispered.

"Perhaps. When I get back to the shop, I'll have a look at it. You never know; I may have to go on a treasure hunt." Sylvia laughed and patted Laura Lee's hand.

"Maybe once you search the desk more, you'll find something else hidden in it."

"I was thinking the same thing myself. I'm having it delivered to the house on Tuesday. I thought it would make a nice addition to the sitting room, rather than taking up space at the shop.

"Well, I better go now; Bill's got the taxi outside waiting for me." She stood and pressed a small kiss on Laura Lee's cheek.

"Bye, bye, honey. Let me know what you find in that diary."

When Sylvia turned to leave, she noted Donald and his mother were not speaking. He was still staring at her.

When he realized, she was staring back, he turned his head slightly and began to speak to his mother again.

Bill drove Sylvia home instead of to her shop; she was tuckered out. Her age was taking a small toll on her. An estate sale and a visit to her sister were all she could take for one day. Considering she was seventy-two, she thought it was a good day.

"Here you go, Miss Sylvia. Home sweet home." Bill opened the taxi door, and she got out.

"Thank you, Bill. I'm tired."

"Well, you get rested up. I'll pick you up in time for church tomorrow."

"Thank you." Sylvia made her way into her house, closed the door and sank into a chair. *First a cup of tea, then an afternoon nap.*

CHAPTER THREE

Monday morning, Sylvia May pushed open the door of the Cup N Cake coffee shop. It was the best place for coffee in town and, luckily, in the same square as her antique store.

"Good morning, Miss Sylvia," Penny Lyle, co-owner of the cupcake and coffee shop, called out. Penny was married to a famous mystery writer named Kyle London. They'd combined his coffee shop and her cupcake shop together when they got married.

"Morning, Penny. What's the special today?" Sylvia glanced around the shop.

Penny held a plate full of lemon poppy seed scones.

"They look yummy. I'll take three to go and my regular cup of coffee." Sylvia opened her purse and pulled out her credit card.

Just then Tricia and Gathe Denver entered the shop. Gathe stepped up behind Sylvia and spoke to her in a friendly tone.

"Hello, Miss Sylvia. How are you today? Did Bill just drop you off?"

Sylvia turned and nodded. "Oh, Gathe. I'm fine, just fine. Yes, Bill left a few minutes ago, got another call."

"Did you get your desk yet?"

"No, I expect it to be delivered tomorrow."

Gathe looked confused. "Wasn't it supposed to be delivered today?"

"Yes, but I changed my mind, decided to have it sent to my house instead. They'll deliver it tomorrow."

"I heard that the Pendecot jewels were lost," Tricia, Gathe's wife, interjected.

Sylvia shook her head. "Yes. That's what I was told."

"And there were no clues left behind?"

"None that I know about, at least not yet. It's not only jewels, but some rare coins are missing, too."

"That sounds intriguing. Tell us more,"

Tricia dropped her voice.

"You want to join us for some coffee?" Gathe asked.

"No, I need to get my shop opened. Hubert promised me the leftovers from the estate sale so I need to make room at the shop. But Tricia, stop by later. I picked up a little something at the estate sale that might hold the answers."

Tricia nodded, and Sylvia turned toward the door. From the corner of her eye, she noted Jennifer and Jason sitting at a small table, holding hands. She realized they had been sitting close enough to overhear her conversation with Gathe and Tricia. Not that it mattered.

"Let me know if you like the scones," Penny called out as Sylvia left the shop and headed to her store. When she reached her door, she stood stock-still. The door was ajar; the window next to the door was broken.

Sylvia stepped back nervously, turned

and scuttled back to Cup N Cake. She hurried through the front door and rushed to where Gathe and Tricia sat.

"Gathe, someone broke into my shop. The window is broken, and the door is open."

Gathe jumped up. "Tricia, call the police." He moved around the table and put his arm around Sylvia. "Now, stay calm. We'll find out what it's all about."

Sylvia stood nervously twisting her hands, waiting while Tricia called 911. As she spoke into her phone and told the police the address and what had happened, Jason and Jennifer looked up.

They both rose from their seats and hurried over. Jennifer spoke up. "We couldn't help but overhear you, Miss Sylvia. Someone broke into your shop?"

"Yes, I was just about to go in when I noticed the window broken and the door ajar. I hope whoever broke in is gone now."

Just then, they heard sirens outside.

They all moved as a group out into the courtyard and waited for the police.

"So, Miss Sylvia," Officer McClan said, while writing on a small notepad. "From what we can tell, someone wanted to steal something specific. It seems only your desk area and the bookshelves were rifled through. Do you have any idea what they were looking for?"

Sylvia shook her head back and forth. Nothing came to mind. Although she had some first edition books, it made no sense for anyone to rifle through her desk.

"Even my safe? Wasn't it broken into?"

The officer shook his head.

Sylvia noticed Jennifer standing alone, Jason had slipped away when the first police car arrived. She walked over and asked, "Jennifer, why did Jason leave?"

Jennifer flushed. "He doesn't like the police. He's afraid that somehow he might be accused of…"

Sylvia lifted Jennifer's hand and patted it. "Your father told me about his juvenile record."

"He's not like that anymore. My father just doesn't understand."

"Give him time. I'm sure Jason will prove himself to your father. Be patient."

Jennifer smiled. "Thank you, Miss Sylvia. I hope nothing important was stolen."

"So, do I, but I've been thinking. If someone was rifling through my desk, they must be looking for something small, like a notebook, or a paper, or a diary."

Jennifer's mouth formed an O. "Do you think so? I know you collect diaries. Do you have any that are worth a lot of money?"

"Hmm, just the newest one, I think." Sylvia's brow furrowed. "Excuse me, Jennifer, I think I need to tell Officer McClan something."

"I noticed a young man here when I first

arrived, but he slipped away before I could ask him any questions," Officer McClan stated.

"Yes, his name is Jason Barnes, but I don't think he has anything to do with the break-in." Sylvia stated.

The officer gave a crooked smile, "Ma'am, I'll be the judge of that. His behavior was odd."

"May I go in the shop now?" Sylvia asked. Her legs were shaking from standing so long. The officer nodded.

"Yes, we need you to take an inventory of everything and tell us if something specific is missing. It may have something to do with that diary, but it could be something else. Where is the diary now?" He asked. She had mentioned it to him earlier.

"It's in my purse. Do I have to turn it in to you?" Sylvia didn't want to have to turn it over, but she would if necessary.

"Not yet, but keep it safe in case I need

it later on."

Sylvia agreed and headed into her shop. She was shocked by the mess. All the papers on her counters were flung on the floor, and all the books in her book corner were tossed around the room. From a quick glance, she could see nothing seriously damaged. With a sigh, she sat on the chair behind her counter and put her head down.

A few minutes later, Bill rushed through the door. "Miss Sylvia, I heard what happened. Are you okay?"

Sylvia lifted her head and gave him a weak smile. "Yes, I'm just feeling a bit overwhelmed." She swung her hand around indicating the mess.

Bill bent over and lifted a book. "I'll take you home then come back here and pick up everything. I may not be able to put the books in order, but I can clean up a bit."

"That's so kind, Bill, but you already do enough, driving me around town. This isn't your mess."

"I'll help," Jennifer's voice rang out as she entered the store. "And, when I find Jason, he'll help, too."

Just then, there was a gasp, and Sylvia's eyes went to the open door again. Hatty was standing there with a hand over her mouth.

"What happened here, Sylvia?" She asked in an unconvincing voice.

Sylvia sighed. "As you can see, Hatty. My shop was broken into."

"Oh, no. Was anything taken?" She glanced around the room and noticed the books strewn about. "Were any of your precious diaries stolen?"

Sylvia shook her head. "I don't think so, but I need to do a full inventory."

"Should I be worried about my shop?" Hatty glanced out the front window. She had a rather distressed look on her face.

"I wouldn't worry, Hatty. It does seem as if they were looking for something specific."

"What's that?"

Bill turned around. "Hatty, Sylvia's pretty shook up right now. Maybe you can come back later?"

Hatty's mouth gaped at Bill's words. "Well, I never..." she pulled her sweater closed across her chest, turned and stomped out of the store. Before she exited, she stopped and looked around once more. "Where is that new desk you bought, Sylvia?"

"It's being delivered to my..." Bill stepped closer, took Hatty by the arm and led her ungraciously to the door. When they reached the door, Hatty pulled away from him, gave one last look around, then huffed away.

Sylvia gave Bill a glare. "Bill, that wasn't very nice."

"She's an old bitty." He walked over and put his arm around Sylvia's shoulders. "Let me take you home."

Sylvia nodded. This mess could wait another day. She was pretty shaky. "If we tape up that broken window, we should be able to leave."

Bill searched for some duct tape and spent a few minutes taping the window. "I'll have to get you a new lock for the front door."

Sylvia slipped her purse on her shoulder and allowed Bill to lead her to the back door. He had parked his taxi on the street behind the antique shop. He insisted Sylvia hold his arm until they reached the car, then he held the car door open so she could slide into the back seat. When he was sure she was settled in, her got into the front seat and turned on the engine.

Bill drove slowly, taking the lovely Gulf Road so Sylvia could relax. He knew she loved the sound of the surf. When he pulled into Sylvia's driveway, he heard her sigh.

"I'm sorry you had to go through all of

that, Sylvia."

"There's nothing to be done about it, but it is disconcerting. I just can't imagine anything in my shop anyone would want so badly. Even my most expensive books aren't worth so much money that anyone would steal them. And besides, why would they have made such a mess?"

Bill eyed her in the mirror. "What about that diary?"

"I can't imagine it's *that* important, even if it has a clue to the whereabouts of Mary Pendecot's jewels. Everyone in town knows I'd be the first to share the information. I wouldn't try to keep them for myself."

Bill's eyes looked dark. "Maybe that's the problem. What if someone doesn't want you to share the information? Maybe you better tell me who all was at that estate sale."

Sylvia leaned forward and opened the taxi door. "I just want to rest now. If you come back in an hour, I'll be ready to go back to the shop and start cleanup."

Bill walked her to the door then patted her hand. "You just get some rest."

CHAPTER FOUR

Sylvia spent the afternoon reorganizing her bookshelves. Nothing was missing, and nothing was damaged. She was happy nothing was gone, but it all seemed so strange. There were some pretty rare editions of books a thief should have taken if it were a robbery.

After an hour or so, she sat down and took a sip of her coffee.

I can't believe my shop was broken into. Is there any chance this was all about that Pendecot Diary?

She reached into her purse and pulled out the diary. She opened to the first page and began to read. Mary Pendecot had started writing in the diary when she first married her husband and moved into the Pendecot mansion.

Sylvia flipped the pages and checked the different entry dates. Mary only wrote in the diary from time to time over twenty years, but the things she wrote about were detailed and filled with rich history.

Sylvia had recently started a blog called "Diaries of the Past." Each day she blogged different excerpts from diaries she'd collected over the years. She already had about 500 followers. Perhaps she would blog the entire Pendecot diary.

Sylvia moved over to her computer and turned it on. First, she would need to pre-blog about it, tell some background details about the Pendecot family, post a photo of the desk and the diary. Maybe she could get back in the house and take some photos.

Hmm, it's going to be very interesting. I'll need to read the Gazette article as well.

A half hour later, the front door opened, and she looked up.

"Doc?"

Doc Holiday stomped into the store. "What's all this hullabaloo I heard about someone breaking into your store?"

Sylvia closed the diary and slipped it into

her purse. She wasn't sure if he noticed it or not. She moved away from the computer. "Yes, someone broke in."

"What'd they take?" His eyes swept the room.

"That's the strange part; nothing's missing."

"Where's that desk you bought the other day?"

"It's not here."

"I can see that," he growled.

Sylvia stood up and stretched. "Doc, what's your interest in that desk?"

The man gave her a mean stare. "I told you, I just like the desk. I came today to make you a fair offer on it."

"But, I don't want to sell it."

"Didn't they make their deliveries today?" He

moved toward the back office and slipped open the door. Sylvia rushed over, pushed him slightly and shut the office door.

"Doc, I'm not interested in selling my desk. I don't need you poking around my office. But seriously, you've never been interested in furniture before. Why this sudden interest in a desk?"

"I told you, I just want to buy it. Why are you being such a stubborn woman?"

Sylvia set her hands on her hips and glared at the man. "I'm not being stubborn. I want to keep the desk. It's not for sale. Now, can you go away so I can finish cleaning up in here?"

The man stomped out the front door, mumbling to himself.

With a small frown on her face, Sylvia wondered, *what does that man want with my desk? It has to be something about the missing coin collection, but I pulled out all the drawers and didn't find any coins.*

Sylvia took a deep breath and turned back to her work, but the bell over the front door chimed.

What now?

Sylvia wiped her hands on a cloth and set it on the counter. She moved to the front of the shop. A young man was standing there.

"Can I help you?" Sylvia called out. The man turned. It was Jason Jones.

"I wanted to know if you could use some help?" His eyes slid around the store. "Jennifer told me to come over and help you."

Without hesitation, Sylvia answered. "That was kind of Jennifer. To tell you the truth, I'm a bit exhausted. I've picked up all the books that were thrown around in disarray, but the whole store needs to have the broken glass swept out. Could you do that?"

"Sure."

Sylvia pointed at the broom against the wall. Jason grabbed it and began to vigorously sweep.

"I'll just push it all to the back door then put it in a trash can. Did you figure out why someone broke in?"

Sylvia shook her head from side to side. "From what I can tell, nothing was taken. I assume it was someone who wanted to go through the desk I bought, but that doesn't explain all my books being thrown on the floor."

Jason glanced around. "Where is that desk?"

Sylvia thought his face showed signs of innocent curiosity, but for right now she didn't feel like giving anyone any more information about the desk. She pretended not to hear his question.

"I've got to go over to Cup N Cake and get a fresh cup of coffee." She waved and left him behind, once more sweeping.

"Hi there, Miss Sylvia." Penny called out.

"Just came to get a refill." Sylvia held up her cup then walked over to the counter. Penny took the cup and began to fill it.

"Sorry to hear about your break-in." Penny spoke sympathetically. "Did they take money?"

"No. Nothing was taken. I thought they'd broken in to steal one of my collectible diaries, but not a single one's missing. All the books were thrown on the floor so it took all day to clean up."

Penny frowned. "It doesn't make much sense. Do you have any thoughts?"

"The only thing I can imagine is that it has something to do with the desk I bought at the Pendecot estate sale. There were several people who seemed overly interested in it, especially since it was in the Gazette."

"But, why would the books be thrown around. Was the desk broken into or damaged?"

Sylvia shrugged her shoulders. "That's the strangest part of all. The desk isn't at my shop. I told Jennifer to have it delivered to my house. It won't be there until tomorrow."

Penny handed the cup to Sylvia. "Well, I

hope it had nothing to do with the desk. The last thing you need is to have your house broken into."

Sylvia's heart dropped. She hadn't thought about that. Maybe she should talk with Officer McClan about it. She'd told him about the diary but hadn't put much emphasis on the desk. Sylvia took her cup and pushed away from the counter.

"I guess it's back to the shop. I closed for the day to clean up the mess. Oh, by the way, can I get a muffin and coffee to go? I'll treat Jason since he's helping me."

"He's a nice young man." Penny pulled a muffin out of the glass case and put it in a bag.

"Hmm, I don't know him, but he offered to help me so I'll give him the benefit of doubt."

"He and Jennifer seem close. But if he can't prove himself, Hubert will never allow Jennifer to keep seeing him."

"I'm just hoping he proves himself to

me," Sylvia grabbed the bag and cups and made her way across the square and back into the antique shop. She noted Hatty's store had several customers.

Not a day to have to be closed. She sighed heavily as she pushed open the front door.

Jason was standing behind the counter. It appeared he was looking at her computer. He stepped back, a startled look on his face.

Sylvia set the coffee cup on the counter, trying to appear casual. She could see Jason had been looking at her website. She handed him the bag with the muffin in it. Not one to beat around the bush, she decided to confront him.

"Jason, I appreciate your helping me around here, but I can see you were on my computer. What's your interest?"

Jason fidgeted with the bottom of his shirt then squared his shoulders. "I didn't mean anything by it. I wanted to check my email. My computer died the other day, but before I could get into my email I saw your blog and started reading about the Pendecot diary. Your blog is really good. I was very interested in what you wrote so far."

Sylvia glared at him, wondering if she should believe him or not.

Jason stepped closer. "Please believe me, Miss Sylvia. I know what they say about me, but you can trust me."

Sylvia took a sip of her coffee, eyeing him over the cup. He looked innocent enough.

She assumed he was a misunderstood young man.

"I'm hoping my followers will enjoy reading a continuing story. I'll post the most interesting excerpts from the Pendecot diary. For all I know, I'll find out the secret hiding place for her jewels."

Jason straightened. "Jewels?"

"Yes, the Pendecot jewels are missing.

They might be hidden in the house somewhere. Since they belonged to Mrs. Pendecot, maybe she wrote about it in the diary."

Jason whistled. "Sounds like a mystery."

Sylvia smiled at the younger man. "There's a muffin in that bag for you." She watched as he eagerly grabbed the bag. "Do you have a job, Jason?"

"No, I've been trying to get one, helping out here and there, but no one will hire me."

"I can use some help. I've been thinking about hiring someone to help me with the bigger items. I'm not able to load items for my customers, and I always have to call Gathe. I don't think he appreciates it, but he's too kind to say anything."

"Do you really mean it, Miss Sylvia? I'm trustworthy. I'll stay out of the way; no one needs to know I'm working here."

Sylvia cocked her head. "Why would I care if anyone knew you were working here?"

A bitter laugh came from the young man's throat. "Seriously, I'm sure you know about my juvenile record. You'd think I was a murderer or bank robber, the way everyone looks at me."

"Psh, you were young and foolish then. I'm willing to give you a try."

Jason picked up the broom again, a huge grin across his face. "Thank you so much, Miss Sylvia. I'll prove valuable to you."

Sylvia looked around at the shop, noting that it seemed as if everything was nearly back in order.

"I'm tired. I think I'll close up shop for tonight. Can you be here at eight thirty each morning.?"

"Yes!" The young man's face lit up.

Sylvia pulled out her cell phone and hit speed dial for the taxi company.

"Bill will be here any minute to pick me up," Sylvia explained after she turned off her cell. "You can hang up your broom for today."

CHAPTER FIVE

"So, you hired him to work for you?" Bill's voice rose in irritation. "Sylvia, he's got a record, and he was behaving in a suspicious manner. What would make you hire him?"

"Oh, you know, keep your enemies near." She chortled slightly. But when she saw the grim line furrow his brow in his rearview mirror, she dropped her eyes. "Really, Bill, I don't think there's anything to worry about. Jason seems to be a very nice young man. I want to give him a chance to prove himself."

"But, you caught him looking at your computer?" Bill kept on.

"He says he was interested in my blog."

Bill steered the taxi into Sylvia's driveway and parked. He got out, came around and opened the door for her.

"I'll walk you in."

"Bill, I'm fine. You don't need to walk me in."

Bill took her hand and placed it into the crook of his. "Miss Sylvia, that break-in doesn't make any sense so until the police figure out who did it, I'll be keeping a closer eye on you. I want to make sure you're safe."

Sylvia smiled. "Alright, Bill. I guess I don't mind."

As they moved up the front walkway to the quaint Cape Cod style home, Bill asked, "Where is the desk you bought?"

Sylvia glanced at him curiously. Bill was never one to ask questions about her purchases. He tended to listen to her talk about things, but he'd never asked a direct question like this before.

"Uhm, it won't be delivered until tomorrow."

"Here? Not the shop?"

"Yes, here. I want to use it myself. It's perfect for my house."

Bill slowly unwrapped a piece of spearmint gum, slid it into his mouth and began to chew on it. He stayed long enough to see Sylvia safely into her house.

The following morning, Bill dropped Sylvia near the courtyard. She stopped in Cup N Cake for her morning coffee then headed towards the antique store. As promised, Jason was leaning against the door. When Sylvia came around the corner, his face lit up.

"Oh, good; you're here." Sylvia handed him her keys and allowed him to open the door.

Jason pushed open the door and allowed Sylvia to enter first.

"We still have some cleaning up to do around here." She announced as she set her purse on the counter and turned around.

"I'll work on that. Why don't you work on that blog? I can't wait to read more."

They spent the rest of the morning i companionable quiet, Sylvia reading a few more entries from the Pendecot diary and then working on the blog. Jason kept himself busy, cleaning and straightening things.

There were several customers that morning, and Sylvia showed Jason how to write up sales and ring them up on the cash register.

"This will be such a help to me. There are times I need to be in the back, and you can wait on the customers."

"I appreciate you giving me this chance, Miss Sylvia."

Sylvia closed the diary and slipped it back into her purse. "Let's go to lunch. By the time we finish, the desk should be arriving at my house. I want to be there to show Hubert where to put it."

Sylvia and Jason sat across from one another at the small corner café. Jason sat enthralled as Sylvia told him some of the stories she'd found in diaries over the last few years.

"I love history. In fact, if I'd gone to college, I would've studied history." His voice dropped.

"Why not go now?"

Jason shook his head. "It's too late now."

"Too late? It's not like you're over the hill or anything. We have a local college; you could start in the fall. You could go part time."

Jason sat quietly for a long time. Sylvia allowed him to mull things over. She pulled out her phone, hit the speed dial, and asked for Bill.

"Bill, I want to get home and be there when the desk is delivered...What time? I think they'll be there by two... oh, you're busy? Oh, okay, I guess I can wait." She ended the call and looked up at Jason.

He must have noted a strange look on her face.

"What's wrong, Miss Sylvia?"

"Nothing, really. It's just that Bill can't

pick me up until about two forty. I'll probably miss Hubert delivering my desk. He knows he can put it in my garage, but I'd hoped to be there."

"That's odd. What did Bill say he was doing?"

"That's just it; he simply said he was busy. Bill's been driving me around for years, and he has never been too busy to come get me. It's never happened before."

"Hmm," Jason finished the last bite of his sandwich. "I'd drive you over, but I only have a scooter." He gave her an endearing smile.

"That's alright. I'll just go later. Can you run the shop when I'm gone?"

"Sure, but I do have something I need to do before then. Can I take off now, and I'll be back to the shop by two thirty? This was something I had scheduled before you gave me the job."

Sylvia agreed and watched Jason scurry out of the café.

Hmm, first Bill's acting strange, and now Jason has to go somewhere and doesn't want to tell me where. Everyone's acting so mysteriously.

"So, Bill, what were you doing that kept you from picking me up earlier?"

Sylvia could see Bill's face in the rearview mirror.

"Uh, nothing, just another fare."

Sylvia noticed him drop his eyes. It was obvious there was something he didn't want to tell her so she just looked out the window and allowed her mind to drift.

When they turned into her driveway, Sylvia was glad to see the delivery van still there. It was backed up to her garage.

When they stopped and Bill opened her door, she slipped out and walked into the garage. The desk had been placed in the middle of the garage floor, but to her dismay, all the drawers were pulled out, a few of them tossed on the floor.

Her hand came up to her mouth as she gasped, "Oh, no!"

Bill stepped into the garage. "What's wrong?" He said, following her gasp, but quickly noted the condition of the desk and its drawers. "Sylvia, step back here." He reached out and pulled her by her arm. But as she turned, her eyes grew larger, and her mouth gaped even wider.

Bill noticed her facial expression change, and his head turned around. He quickly pulled Sylvia against his chest.

"Don't look, Sylvia. Let's get out of here; we need to call the police."

They both stumbled out of the garage. Bill pulled out his cell phone and dialed 911.

"Is he dead? We should check; maybe he's just hurt." Sylvia moaned.

Bill opened the taxi door and pressed Sylvia to sit down. "I'll check on him, but you stay here."

Sylvia sat quietly, twisting her fingers

nervously. She looked down at her purse and noticed the diary sticking out.

Just then Bill opened the taxi door. His face spoke volumes.

"Dead?" Sylvia croaked.

He nodded. Sylvia thought his face was a bit pale, and his hands were shaking.

"How?" Sylvia pleaded.

Bill shook his head. "I think he was shot."

"Who, who... is it?"

Bill's head dropped, and his answer sounded as if it were being ripped from his soul. "Hubert!"

CHAPTER SIX

"Tell me, Miss Sylvia, everyone you think would have known that the desk was being delivered today."

Sylvia sat on the couch in her house. Bill handed her a glass of ice water; but after the first sip, she set it on the coffee table.

"I'm too shook up to hold the glass steady."

Officer McClan flipped open his notebook and sat on a hardback chair across from Sylvia.

"Well, let me see. I told Jennifer, Hubert's daughter, to have it delivered to my house. I told my sister Laura Lee about it. As a matter of fact, there was someone there who overheard my conversation."

"Who was that?"

Sylvia thought for a moment. "His first name was Donald. I'm not sure of his last name."

"Was he a resident?"

"No, he was visiting his mother. He was

big with black hair. I don't remember anything else about him."

McClan nodded. "We can find out who he is. Anyone else?"

"Gathe and Tricia Denver, Jason Barnes and Bill."

The officer wrote all the names down and told her he would follow up with each of them. As they were finishing up, a car pulled into the driveway. Gathe and Tricia both got out and rushed to the porch, opened the door and came in.

"Sylvia, oh my! We were worried about you."

Sylvia's head popped up.

"Why were you worried about her?" Officer McClan asked.

"We heard about... the... well, I guess the only thing to say is, the murder."

Officer McClan stood and faced the couple. "Just how did you hear about it, may I ask?"

Tricia cocked her head sideways. "This is

a small town."

"Yes, but I've only been here forty-five minutes. How could you possibly know anything?" He glared at them.

Gathe stepped forward and pushed Tricia behind him. "Officer, if there's one thing I know about this town, it's the gossip chain. From what I can imagine, Bill must have called his dispatcher to say he couldn't work the rest of the evening. The dispatcher, I think her name is Janice Wardon, must have quizzed him, and he probably gave in and told her all about it. Janice then called her mother. Her mother is the head of the prayer chain from our church. I figure four or five others were called and given the information to pass on before Tricia got the call. But I assure you, Officer, we didn't pass the information on. We closed shop and rushed right over here to see if we could do anything for Miss Sylvia."

Tricia peaked out from behind Gathe

and bobbed her head up and down.

Officer McClan's lips pressed together for a moment, then he said, "Miss Sylvia was telling me who knew about the desk being delivered. You are both on the list."

Gathe moved closer to Officer McClan and glanced at the list of names.

"Uhm, there are a few more names you need to add to that list."

Sylvia looked up with a questioning look.

"After Sylvia told me about the desk being delivered to her house on Tuesday, she realized her shop had been robbed. Well, needless to say, it was the talk of the day. Later on, I went for a cup of coffee at Cup N Cake, and everyone was discussing what happened. Doc Holiday was there, and somehow the conversation got around to the desk Miss Sylvia bought, and, well... I guess I told him she was having it delivered to her house instead of the shop."

Gathe's shoulders sagged, and he ran a

hand through his hair. "I'm really sorry, Miss Sylvia."

Sylvia pushed herself up to a standing position. "That's alright, Gathe. I know how things get around in this town. But do you think Doc would shoot a man just to get to the desk?"

"Or smash him over the head?" Officer McClan interjected. They all stared at him in wonder. "Yes, the ambulance team informed me that Hubert had been hit on the head pretty hard before he was shot."

They were all silent for several moments, then officer McClan cleared his throat. "You said there were a few more names to add to the list. So far, you've only mentioned Doc Holiday."

Tricia stepped forward at this point. "There was a woman, I didn't know her, but Gathe said she had been at the Pendecot estate sale. She spoke to you at the sale, Sylvia."

Sylvia thought for a minute. "Alice

Pendecot?"

Officer McClan wrote the name down. "She doesn't live in Harbor Inn, does she?"

"I don't think so. She told me she used to come visit her grandmother when she was young. But she also told me she was leaving town the next day."

"We'll check the Inn and other hotels. If she's still in town, we'll locate her."

"Officer, has Hubert's body been taken away yet?"

"Yes, Ma'am."

"And the desk?"

"My men have photographed it and looked it over pretty well. I don't think we need to take it to headquarters."

"Can I have it moved inside?"

Officer McClan nodded and closed his notebook. "We'll leave now, but I'll have an officer drive by once an hour for the next few days. However, if there was something in that desk that anyone wanted, I'm pretty sure they got it already."

Sylvia cringed, once more thinking of the diary. But Officer McClan didn't feel the diary was significant enough for anyone to have killed someone for it.

CHAPTERR SEVEN

Bill sat beside Sylvia, patting her hand. He waited for her to speak.

"Oh, Bill. I can't believe someone killed Hubert. Sure, he was a bit gruff, but who would want him dead?"

"I'm not sure anyone wanted him dead. It seems to me that desk is the problem. From the looks of it, someone basically ripped it apart looking for something."

"That's true, but if it's not the desk, then we have to consider other options. For example, Gathe and Hubert have been in competition..."

Bill squeezed her hand. "Sylvia, you know Gathe. He's a good, Christian man. There isn't any chance he killed Hubert."

Sylvia's head slumped with a slight nod, "Of course he couldn't have done anything like this. I'm just so confused and upset. Has anyone told Jennifer yet?"

Suddenly her eyes popped open, and her mouth formed an O. "Bill, you don't think Jason could have done this? You know he took off work early today, and he and Hubert didn't get along."

Bill glared at her. "You can't have it both ways, Sylvia. You just hired him because you felt you could trust him. Now you're questioning it?"

"You're right. I told myself I was going to trust Jason, give him a chance. Just pretend I never said anything."

"Listen, Sylvia. I think you need to have someone come and stay with you. Since Laura Lee is gone to the nursing home, I'm not comfortable leaving you alone."

"Oh, Bill, that's just silly."

"No, it's not. As a matter of fact, I think I'll be the one. I can stay in Laura Lee's room until this thing is solved."

Sylvia smiled. "I won't argue with you, Bill. I have to admit, I don't want to be alone. It's so foolish, to be my age and be afraid of being alone."

"No problem. I'll just head home and

gather up an overnight bag. For now, I'll take you to the shop. Jason should be there."

Sylvia allowed Bill to help her to the taxi. She didn't want to go back home until the police had taken care of Hubert's body.

When they reached her shop, Sylvia went in the back door. Jason was at the front counter. His head turned.

"Hi, Miss Sylvia. Did you get the desk?"

Sylvie stopped; her jaw dropped. The look on Jason's face changed.

"What's wrong? You look upset."

"You haven't heard from Jennifer?"

Jason shook his head, "No... what?"

Sylvia walked further into the store, reached out and placed her hand on top of Jason's. She hated having to be the one to tell him.

"I'm sorry, I have some bad news. When Hubert delivered the desk today, someone shot and killed him in my garage."

Jason gasped. He lifted his hand to

swipe his bangs off his face. His hand was trembling. "Has anyone told Jennifer yet?"

"The police have probably been there by now."

"Miss Sylvia, I think I should go to her. She's going to be pretty upset." He straightened and began to walk towards the back of the store.

"Okay, Jason. But listen. The police are going to want to ask you questions as well."

"Me? Why?"

"Because I told them you were one of the people who knew the desk was being delivered today. And, well, you did sort of disappear when my desk was being delivered."

"So, I'm the prime suspect? It figures. All I was doing was visiting my probation officer. Not that I'm even on probation. He's just a friend, but it doesn't sound very good to tell people about him. It was his birthday today."

"Just tell the police that. I'm sure your friend can vouch for you. It will all be okay. But, Jason. It takes time for people to trust. You just keep working here for me, and after a few months, no one will even remember you ever had a record."

Jason didn't look like he believed her, but he rushed out of the shop to head over to be with Jennifer.

Sylvia sat at the counter, her head in her hands, trying to make sense of the whole thing.

What about Jennifer? she thought. *Could she have had a grudge against her father?* Sylvia could not believe her own thoughts. Jennifer was like any other rebellious daughter, but she truly loved her father. There was no way she would have done anything to hurt him.

Lord, please help me to understand what happened. Why would anyone want to kill Hubert?

Sylvia opened her computer, pulled up a spreadsheet document and began to make a list of everyone who knew about the desk being delivered. Beside the name, she wrote a reason why she thought they would want to either kill Hubert or search the desk.

But, what about the break-in at my shop? Could that have something to do with it. Perhaps the same person broke into the shop first. If that's the case, then it wasn't the desk they were interested in. It had to be something that might've been inside the desk.

The diary? It was the only thing she could imagine. She had basically searched the entire desk herself, and that was all she'd found in it.

Hmm, time to do some more reading. I need to know if there's something in that diary someone would kill for.

For the next hour, Sylvia read from the diary, making a new post on the website when she was done. It crossed her mind that someone who read her blog might be interested in getting hold of the diary, but she had changed the names a bit so it didn't seem likely.

The front door bell jingled, and Sylvia looked up. Hatty entered the shop.

"Hello, Hatty. Can I help you?"

The woman rushed across the store. "Oh, Sylvia. I've been so worried. I heard about Hubert. Is it true? He was killed in your garage?"

Sylvia swallowed. She didn't really want to talk about Hubert's death.

"What's that you're working on?" Hatty's eyes were riveted on the diary.

Sylvia slammed it shut and placed it in her purse. "Just working on my blog."

"Your blog?"

"Yes, I have a blog. I put some of the excerpts from diaries I acquire on it. People seem to be very interested in it."

"Hmm, a blog. Perhaps my grandson

could help me start one. You know, post photos of items I have in my shop. Tell the history of them."

"That sounds like a wonderful idea. I appreciate you coming over, but I don't have any other information about Hubert's death to share."

Hatty, her mind now set on writing a blog of her own, turned abruptly and left the store without saying another word.

Sylvia stood and stretched. She decided she'd head over to Cup N Cake to get another lemon poppy seed muffin. She grabbed her purse but decided not to take the diary with her. Still, she couldn't leave it just lying around. She slipped the diary out of her purse and placed it in her small safe and twisted the dial. Then she locked the shop's door and strolled casually across the courtyard, taking time to glance in the windows of the other shops.

"Hi, Sylvia," Penny's pleasant voice called out when Sylvia stepped into Cup N

Cake.

"Hi, Penny. I'll take a lemon poppy seed." She moved across the room and sat down. She quickly scanned the room, the only other person in the shop had her back to them. However, the door opened, and Hatty came in.

"Oh, Sylvia. I thought you were at your shop working on that diary. By the way, where did you get that one from?"

Sylvia scowled, "That's none of your business!"

"I didn't realize everything was such a secret. Is that why you stuck it in your purse so quickly when I came in?"

Sylvia didn't answer. She glared at the woman.

"Oh, well, excuse me." Hatty turned and ordered a blueberry scone. She tapped her fingers on the counter impatiently while she waited. Sylvia stared at her, irritation apparent on her face. From the corner of her eye, she noted the door close behind the person who had been sitting in the shop.

After eating her muffin, Sylvia returned to the Good Old Days Antique Store. She spent the next hour putting some books, which had been delivered that morning, out on the shelves. Several times she had to step into the back room. She had a few customers come in the shop and actually sold several antiques and two rare books.

At the end of the day, Bill arrived with a big grin.

"So, a quiet day?"

Sylvia nodded. "Yes. Except for the third degree I got from Hatty."

"The old bitty," Bill grumbled.

"She's not even as old as I am, Bill." Sylvia crossed her arms over her chest and glared at him.

Bill laughed and took her arm and tucked it into the crook of his then led her out to the car.

Once she was settled on the seat and

Bill slipped in the front seat, she put her head back for a moment, then gasped slightly. "I forgot my purse, Bill! The back-door locks automatically."

Bill turned with a frown. "How will we get in? If you left your purse inside, your keys are in there."

Sylvia sat up. "I keep a spare key out back, in a hide-a-rock. It's right over there." Sylvia pointed at a large grey rock, sitting next to the garbage cans, outside her shop's door.

Bill got out of the taxi, walked around the car and picked up the rock. He turned it over and retrieved the key. In seconds, he disappeared into the shop.

Sylvia waited, but after five minutes, she slid out of the car and stepped into the shop.

"Bill?" She called.

"Sylvia, I can't find your purse anywhere."

"What!!!" Sylvia moved toward her

counter. She searched the area. Even bent down and looked far into the corner. It was too dark to see anything.

"Let me flip on the lights." Bill moved toward the wall. Sylvia felt around. Finally, Bill must have found the light switch and turned them on because she could see much better, but her purse was nowhere to be seen.

Sylvia straightened. "Bill, I can't find my purse. I know I put it on the counter."

Bill stared at her.

"Oh goodness. That means someone came in my shop today and stole my purse."

"You're kidding! First the store was broken into, then a man was murdered in your garage, and now your purse is missing. It's just plain crazy."

Sylvia patted his arm. "No, Bill. It just means that we know what the intruder is looking for. It has to be the diary. And whoever it was thought it was in my shop, then they decided it was in the desk still and killed Hubert looking for it. But, they finally realized I had to have it so they stole my purse."

Bill pulled out his cell phone and dialed 911. After he explained the situation to the dispatcher, he disconnected.

"So, this person, whoever it was, has the diary now?"

Sylvia shook her head. "No. I put it in the safe."

Bill blew out a breath. "Okay, let's get it out and give it to the police so that we won't have any more problems. Once they figure out who did this, you can get the diary back."

Sylvia agreed. While they waited for the police, she pulled the diary out of the safe. She flipped through several pages, reading as fast as she could, hoping to get a clue to what the intruders were looking for, but when the police arrived she hadn't discovered anything.

"So, you really believe this is all about the diary?" a young officer asked.

"Yes, it has to be. And that's why Hubert was killed."

The young man looked skeptical but said he would call it in. He stepped outside to make the call. After a few minutes, he returned.

"Miss Sylvia, I just spoke to Officer McClan. He assures me this has nothing to do with the diary. They just arrested the person they think murdered Hubert."

Sylvia's eyes opened wider. Her hand touched her heart. "Who...who was it?"

"Doc Holiday."

CHAPTER EIGHT

"Doc Holiday?" Sylvia couldn't believe what she was hearing. "Why would Doc kill anyone?" she asked Officer McClan when he arrived at her shop.

"We went to talk to him because he was on your list. When we got there, we found the coins from the Pendecot estate. It was obvious; he must have found them in the desk."

Sylvia shook her head back and forth. Doc was an old humbug and loved coin collecting, but murder? Never!

"What did he tell you?"

"We haven't had time to interrogate him yet, but it looks like it will be an open and shut case."

Sylvia turned to Bill, "This isn't right. We have to go and talk to him. There has to be an explanation."

Bill tried to soothe her by gently stroking her arm and speaking in a low tone.

"Sylvia, sit down; you're all upset. You

should go home and get some rest."

"No, we have to talk to Doc." She looked at Officer McClan. "Will we be allowed to speak to him?"

The man's eyebrows drew together, "No, Miss Sylvia. But we will give him a chance to explain everything. Once we know more, we will let you know."

The officer turned to leave. Sylvia stood with the diary dangling from her hand, a scowl on her face.

"Bill, what can we do?" Sylvia sat down at her counter.

"I don't know. I guess we have to wait."

"You know I'm not one to sit around and wait." She slumped her shoulders. After a few moments, Sylvia sat up.

"That Coast Drive Mile Long Yard Sale is next month. I have to get busy boxing up items and doing inventory."

"Are you going to set up on the coast?"

"Sure, I'll leave Jason here to pick up any stragglers who actually make it to town.

People start on one end and walk the whole mile. If you don't have a table near the beginning or middle, you don't sell much because most people are tired or already carrying full bags."

Bill moved closer and leaned on the counter. "Hmm, you know I have an old golf cart. Maybe if I set up a few tables before you, I could offer to drive people back to their cars to drop off their packages then bring them back. That way, they'd have free hands to start all over again at your table."

A huge smile spread across Sylvia's face. "Bill, that's a wonderful idea. Why are you always so good to me?"

"You're my favorite passenger."

Sylvia laughed. "I'm almost your only passenger."

Bill nodded then straightened up. "Do you still want to go home?"

"No, Bill. I'd rather work while we wait to hear from the police. Why don't you go back to work? I'll call you if I hear anything."

Bill shuffled around the room. "I guess, now that they have Doc, you should be safe." He tried to sound assured, but she could tell he was still worried. Neither of them really believed Doc Holiday could be the killer.

An hour later, Jason came back into the shop.

"Oh, Jason, how is Jennifer?"

He ran a hand through his hair. "She's pretty torn up. I would have stayed with her, but she had to go down to the morgue. She wanted to go alone."

Sylvia tsked. "That will be awful for her."

"Yes, but she insisted on going alone. She said she had to make the funeral arrangements."

Just then, the front door opened, and Hatty rushed in. "Sylvia! Sylvia, did you hear they think Doc Holiday killed

Hubert?"

Jason gasped. "They know who did it?"

Sylvia reached over and patted his hand. Her voice dropped. "They found the Pendecot coins. Doc had them. So, they think he killed Hubert."

Jason's face turned red in anger.

"Bill and I don't believe he did it. There has to be some other explanation. We're waiting to hear from the police." Sylvia looked up at Hatty with a frown. "Hatty, are you setting up a table in the Coast Drive Mile Long Yard Sale?"

"Goodness, no. It will be too hot outside for me. I'm sure I'll sell plenty from the shop that weekend." Suddenly, she turned and gave Sylvia a suspicious look. "Are you?"

"Yes, Hatty. Not many customers come to the shops that weekend. They stick to the tables on the street. If you want to get a space next to mine, we can take turns helping one another, you know, if we need bathroom breaks or time to eat."

Hattie stood with her mouth hanging open. "Well, Sylvia. That is a nice offer."

"Besides, I have an extra tent you can borrow. It blocks the sun and protects you from rain."

"So, you'll close your shop completely?"

Sylvia hesitated. "No, I hired Jason to work here for me. He'll stay here and run the shop."

Hatty bit her bottom lip. "Hmm. I suppose I can try to find someone to run my shop that weekend." She glanced at Jason with a frown as if trying to place him. She leaned closer to him and asked, "Do you have any friends who might work for me?"

Jason pulled his head back and stared at her. "No, sorry. I don't have many friends here. I usually only hang around with Jennifer."

"Hubert's daughter?"

"Yes."

Hatty looked as if she were about to say something more, but Sylvia stepped silently between them. "Jason, can you take these empty boxes to the back room?" She pushed a small pile of boxes towards him.

Jason straightened and plodded from the room.

Hatty's eyes followed him. "Sylvia, I've heard things about that young man."

"Most not true," Sylvia insisted. "Hatty, I've got things to do."

"Okay, Sylvia. If you hear any more about Doc, please let me know."

Sylvia nodded and watched the other woman walk out of the store.

When Jason came back to the front, he scanned the room. "Miss Hatty gone?"

"Yes, Jason. I'm sorry about that. She's a real busybody."

"Nothing I'm not used to. This town... these people... well, they're never going to accept me."

"Yes, they will. It's just going to take time."

"But now that Hubert's dead, everyone will be even more suspicious."

"Not if Doc killed him."

Jason slumped his shoulders. "You don't think he did it, and I agree. When they finally figure that out, I'll be next in line as a suspect."

Sylvia didn't answer.

Sylvia spent the rest of the afternoon reading the Pendecot diary and upgrading her blog. She kept Jason busy, but they didn't speak any further about Doc Holiday.

Bill showed up at the end of the day and helped Sylvia into his cab.

"Need a nice quiet ride before you go home?"

"No, but I better stop by and see Laura Lee before the end of the day. If she heard anything about Doc Holiday, she might be upset."

Bill drove straight to the nursing home and walked Sylvia in to the front waiting area.

"I'll just sit out on the front rocking chairs and wait for you."

Sylvia gave him a gracious smile. "Thank you, Bill. I can always rely on you. I shouldn't be too long."

Sylvia moved further down the hallway. Her sister was not in the sitting area. Sylvia found her in her room.

"Laura Lee, what are you doing in your room? I thought I saw them setting up for Bingo down in the main area."

Laura Lee glanced up at Sylvia but, for a few seconds, didn't seem to recognize her.

Sylvia's brow drew together. She knew these moments would come and go and, eventually, Laura Lee might not recognize her at all. She just wasn't prepared for it yet.

Finally, Laura Lee's face lit up. "Sylvia

May!"

Sylvia moved across the room and sat on the edge of the bed. Laura Lee was in a wheelchair. Sylvia took her sister's hand and patted it. "Yes, Dear, it's me."

They spoke of general things for a while. Sylvia checked the closet to make sure Laura Lee had plenty of clean clothes. She peeked at the sheets on the bed to make sure they had been changed properly.

"Is there anything I can get you from home or the store, Laura Lee?"

The other woman thought for a few moments. "I would love some of those lemon poppy seed muffins from Cup N Cake."

Sylvia laughed. "Yes, I know you love them. I'll bring you a big tin full tomorrow."

"Oh, Sylvia. I've wanted to tell you something. One of my friends here has lost her son."

Sylvia cocked her head and glanced at

her sister. "What do you mean?"

"Just what I said. His name is Donald, and he comes to see his mother every single day. But he hasn't been here in two days. She says she has called him and even asked her younger brother to go check on him, but he's not anywhere around."

Sylvia remembered the man. She also recalled how he had overheard her talking about the desk and the diary.

"I'll tell Officer McClan about it. Now, let's get you out to the Bingo game." She pushed her sister's wheelchair slowly down the hallway and settled her at her place.

Sylvia thought about bringing up the death of Hubert, but she decided against it. She didn't want to upset her sister.

"Well, Dear. I've got Bill waiting on the front porch so I'll leave you to your game. I hope you win."

Laura Lee snickered. "I hope I don't win. All the prizes are knickknacks to display in our rooms, they say. With everything I brought from home, I don't have room for any more little things."

Sylvia nodded in understanding. "I'll try to come up with an idea to suggest for different types of prizes. Maybe coupons for some of the local bakeries, or something else."

Laura Lee grinned. "That sounds like a good idea. If we win the coupons, we can give them to our families to pick up some goodies for us."

"Okay. I'll be back tomorrow, and I'll bring you some lemon poppy seed muffins."

Before Sylvia could turn away, Laura Lee waved her closer and pointed at the woman sitting at the table behind her.

"That's the one who lost her son."

Sylvia noted the sad expression on the woman's face.

"I'll call Officer McClan as soon as I get home."

CHAPTER NINE

Sylvia stood in the garage, staring at the desk. Although the drawers were all pulled out, it wasn't damaged, with the exception of one panel, which had been pried off.

That must have been where the coins were hidden.

She bent over and lifted the drawers one at a time and slid them into the desk.

Once in the house, Sylvia made a call to Jason and to Gathe Denver. They both agreed to come over the next day and help her move the desk into the house.

After a small bowl of potato soup and a salad, Sylvia prepared for bed. The image of the desk seemed to haunt her. Suddenly, she realized what was bothering her.

The person must have known where the coins were, or more than just that one panel would have been pried off. Whoever did it wasn't looking for the diary, only the coins.

Sylvia called the number Officer McClan had given her. She spoke to him about Donald's disappearance, and she shared her thoughts about the person who stole the coins.

"Have you been able to get Doc to admit to killing Hubert?"

"No, Miss Sylvia. The more I talk to him, the less I believe he could've killed him. The coroner said that Hubert was hit over the head with something first. Doc's got a pretty debilitating old shoulder injury."

Sylvia sat on the edge of her bed. "Hmm. What does Doc say?"

"He swears he bought the coins from someone. Had no idea they were the Pendecot coins."

"But whom does he say he bought them from?" She asked the officer.

"He said it was a tall, dark haired man."

Sylvia tried to picture everyone she had seen the day of the estate sale. "Officer, that sounds like Donald. The man whose mother said he is missing."

Officer McClan assured Sylvia they would look a little harder for Donald.

Sylvia finally settled in for the night, running different scenarios through her mind. The image of Donald killing Hubert didn't ring true either.

"And may I have a box of lemon poppy seed muffins?" Sylvia asked Penny the next morning. "Laura Lee just loves them."

"Of course. How is she doing, by the way?"

Sylvia's smile disappeared. "Slipping."

Penny's hand covered her mouth, "I'm so sorry."

"She's old. In fact, she and I are both old."

"You'll never be old, Sylvia." Kyle, Penny's husband joked as he stepped into the Cup N Cake shop.

"I don't know, I'm feeling every bit of my age, especially since Hubert was killed in my garage." She rolled her neck to relieve the tenseness.

Kyle nodded. "Have you heard anything more about Doc Holiday?"

Sylvia sat at a table, Kyle brought her a cup of coffee and sat beside her.

"I don't think Doc did it. Officer McClan said he didn't have the strength to hit Hubert over the head, and someone *did* hit him over the head."

Kyle whistled. "I thought he was shot."

"Yes, but first he was hit over the head."

Penny stepped up with the box of muffins. "Here you go, Sylvia. I hope Laura Lee enjoys them:

"Have you spoken to Jennifer?" Sylvia asked.

Their faces took on a look of sympathy. "I stayed with her last night," Penny explained.

"Does she have any idea what she is going to do now?"

"I think she and Gathe are going to

combine businesses."

"Hmm," Sylvia murmured.

"People might think he killed Hubert, just to get Hubert's business." Kyle's voice dropped. "It won't be very nice around here until the real killer is caught."

"Miss Sylvia, do you want this pile of books in a box or on the shelf?" Jason's enthusiastic voice called out.

Sylvia poked her head out of the back room. "Box them up and put them in the pile of items we're taking to the Mile-Long Yard Sale.

Jason grabbed the books and whistled as he worked.

"You sound happy," Sylvia noted.

"I am."

"Why?"

"Because Jennifer has agreed to be my girlfriend." A wide grin split his face.

"Now, isn't that nice?"

Jason stopped for a moment with a

frown. "It's great, except people might think I killed Hubert to get Jennifer to start dating me. But I can't worry about that. She needs me now more than ever."

Sylvia gave a small nod and returned to the back room, but Jason peeked into the back and asked, "Why aren't you working on the blog today?"

"I left the diary at home by mistake. I was reading in bed last night."

"Have you found any hint in it about the lost jewels?"

"Nothing. Last night I read about the first-time Alice Pendecot came to visit her grandmother. She was seven years old." Sylvia smirked. "She must have been a real handful. Mrs. Pendecot wrote about how the girl was always getting into her jewelry box, taking the shiny things out and trying them on. However, the child never wanted to return them."

Jason laughed. "Girls sure do like jewelry. As a matter of fact, I'm thinking of buying a piece of jewelry for Jennifer. What do you think?"

Sylvia placed her hands on her hips. "I don't think you should do that so soon. Jennifer likes you. When it gets closer to her birthday or Christmas, then think about jewelry."

"Okay, Miss S. I'll do what you say. Now, I'm going over to meet Jennifer for lunch, if that's okay with you."

"Sure, sure. Go along. I'll just eat my sandwich in the back room today.

Jason tramped across the room, swung open the front door and slammed it behind him.

Goodness, it will take me a while to get used to having young people around again.

Ugh, Sylvia set down the tuna sandwich and pushed it away. *I just can't get the recipe right. Only Laura Lee knew how to make a good tuna sandwich.*

Sylvia sighed and bent over to push some crumbs off the desk into the garbage. As she straightened, she thought she heard a creaking sound come from behind.

She started to stand and turn, all at the same time; but suddenly an excruciating pain shot through her head, and the room went black.

Sylvia tried to open her eyes, but her head was pounding. A slow moan came from her lips.

Someone grabbed her hand. "Miss Sylvia, I'm here."

She turned her head slowly and focused on Bill's face. "What??? What happened?"

"Someone hit you over the head."

Sylvia tried to push herself up to a sitting position, but her head swam. She slipped back down.

"Where am I?" She scanned the room slowly. "The hospital?"

"Yes. When Jason came back from lunch, he found you in the back room. He called an ambulance then got hold of me."

Sylvia tried to remember anything from earlier. The image of tuna fish filled her mind.

"Why did someone hit me? Were they trying to kill me?" Sylvia turned worried eyes to Bill.

"No, believe it or not. Someone stole your purse."

The women's eyes opened wide. "My purse. Oh, Bill, it has to be the diary. There wasn't anything else in my purse."

"So, you think the diary is gone? Good. Now maybe all this craziness will stop." Bill slapped his leg.

Sylvia tilted her head. "Sorry, Bill, but I still have the diary. I left it at home today."

A moan poured from Bill's lips.

CHAPTER TEN

Sylvia was sitting up in the hospital bed. A somber Jennifer pushed Laura Lee's wheelchair into the room.

"Hello, Laura Lee." Sylvia called out, the other woman's eyes riveted on her sister.

"Oh, I've been so worried, Sylvia. When I heard you were hurt, I didn't know what to do. I'm so thankful this young woman came and got me."

Jennifer flopped into a chair. "It's the least I could do since you've been so kind to Jason, Miss Sylvia."

"How is Jason?"

The girl waved a hand airily. "He's great. He loves the job at your antique shop, and he and Gathe have been talking about estate sales. I think Jason might have finally found his niche. It's just too bad he didn't find it before my father died. They could have at least had one thing in common."

"Jennifer, they had you in common, and

their love for you."

The girl flushed slightly, but Sylvia could tell the comment made her a little happier. Jennifer stood and moved to the door.

"I'll just let you ladies talk. I'll be back in a half hour."

Sylvia watched as the girl disappeared down the hallway. Then she turned to her sister.

"How are you, Laura Lee?"

"I'm fine. But what about you."

"I'm better. I'll go home tomorrow. I can tell you, though, it's not nice being hit over the head."

Laura Lee squinted at her sister. "Who do you think did it? Doc Holiday?"

"No, he was still being held at the police station. Officer McClan thinks this might mean Doc wasn't the one who killed Hubert."

Laura Lee's eyes drifted across the room for a moment. "Did you tell the officer about Donald? He's still missing."

"Yes, and Officer McClan is worried about his disappearance. It's too much of a coincidence, him missing at the same time Hubert was killed and then I was hit over the head."

"Oh, I hope it wasn't Donald who did those things. His mother has no one else to rely on. It would be awful for her if he was put in jail."

Sylvia nodded slowly. The movement still hurt. "Unfortunately, Jason informed the police he saw a tall, dark haired man near my shop around the time I was hit. It might've been Donald."

A week later, Sylvia was finally able to work a half day at her shop. She still had a slight headache, but other than that, she felt fine.

"Jason, you did a great job while I was away." Sylvia patted him on the back.

"I'm really enjoying it, Miss S. I've been talking to Gathe Denver, and he wants me to work some of the estate sales with him as well."

"I'm glad, Jason. Antiques aren't for everyone, especially not many young people; but if you enjoy them, it's very satisfying."

The young man nodded. "I've never been interested in anything before. Jennifer thinks I've finally found my niche."

As they spoke, the front door opened, and a man stepped into the store. He had a baseball cap pulled down in front of his eyes. Sylvia was about to stroll over and speak to him but suddenly gasped.

She quickly turned and rushed into the back room, picked up her phone and dialed Officer McClan's number. After a whispered conversation, she ended the conversation and moved back to the front.

Jason was talking to the man. Sylvia stood to the side, listening.

The man leaned against the counter. "So, I was wondering if this shop purchased anything from the Pendecot estate sale?"

Jason's eyebrow rose. "Uhm, nothing for the shop. But I think Hubert had promised to send some things over here. Right now, they're all boxed up in the back of Hubert's garage."

The man nodded and turned as if to leave the store. Sylvia stepped closer to him.

"Excuse me. I couldn't help overhear your conversation with Jason. You're interested in things from the Pendecot estate?"

"Yep, wondered if there were any pieces of furniture, you know, end tables and things like that?"

Sylvia was trying to keep the man from leaving her shop. "No, I didn't get anything like that, but I have other end tables that are nice over in this corner. May I show them to you?"

The man looked at her impatiently. "No.

I'm only interested in items from the Pendecot estate."

Sylvia dropped her shoulders. "I'm sorry I don't have anything from it, except a desk. I did buy a desk. It's not here; it's at my house. Are you interested in a desk?"

The man shifted from one foot to another. "No, I alr... no, I'm not interested in a desk."

Sylvia leaned over and spoke in what could only be called a conspirator's voice. "Did you hear about the Pendecot coins? It seems they were hidden inside the desk I bought. But someone stole them." She turned innocent eyes towards the man.

"And, whoever stole them, killed Hubert," Jason's voice interrupted. The man stiffened.

"The police arrested Doc Holiday because he has the coins, but none of us believe he did it."

"Well, if you don't have anything from the estate..." the man turned and moved toward the door.

Sylvia chewed her bottom lip.

As the man reached out for the knob, the door was pushed open from the outside, and Officer McClan stepped through the door.

The dark-haired man stopped in shock, turned as if to bolt out the back way, but Officer McClan's hand fell heavily on his shoulder.

"Not so fast, Donald. We've been looking for you."

"Me?" the man squeaked, trying to pull away.

"Yes, you. You are a person of interest in the death of one of our town's favorite men, Hubert."

Donald's eyes grew large. "No way; you can't pin murder on me."

McClan stepped closer until he was almost face to face with the man.

"Alright, if not murder, what then?"

"I stole the coins. I sold them to Doc

Holiday."

Sylvia sat down behind the counter. Her legs felt like Jell-O. She stared at the two men.

McClan cleared his throat. "Basically, that's an admission of guilt. If you stole the coins from the desk, then you must have been the one to hit Hubert over the head and then shoot him.

"No, no, no. You don't understand." The man sputtered. "I... I heard the old ladies talking about the coins so I looked up that article and saw the desk. I did some research on old desks and where things might be hidden. I knew when the desk was going to be delivered so I was there waiting."

Jason pressed forward, anger on his face. "You scum, you killed my girlfriend's father."

"No, I didn't. I snuck up behind him and knocked him on the head with a pipe I brought. He was fine, even moaning a bit.

I looked over the desk and found a small cranny that could be pried open. The coins were there."

Officer McClan looked skeptical. "So, you want us to believe someone else came along and shot him?" His brows drew together.

The man's hands were shaking as he reached up, took the baseball cap off then resettled it on his head. "That's exactly what I'm trying to say. Right after I found the coins, the man started to push himself up so I grabbed the loot and took off. I cut through the back yard. I didn't go back out front to the van so I didn't see anyone else, but I heard a shot. Needless to say, I was terrified. After I sold the coins to Doc, I went into hiding."

Sylvia sat up straight and asked. "Why come here today then?"

"I remembered hearing about some jewels being missing or lost. I figured if the coins were hidden in the desk, the jewels were probably hidden in a piece of furniture like an end table or a bureau. I already asked at Blue Willow Antiques, but she told me that anything left from the sale was going to be given to the owner of this store." The man's whole demeanor slumped. "I swear, I'm not a murderer."

Office McClan pulled his handcuffs out. "If you come along peacefully, I won't cuff you. But for now, you will be held on theft and maybe suspicion of murder."

Donald's wild eyes sought Sylvia. "Will you keep an eye on my mother? She's going to be so worried. They take good care of her there, but..."

Sylvia walked over and patted his hand. "Yes, Donald. I'll check on her every time I go see Laura Lee."

The man nodded gratefully and followed Officer McClan out the front door.

When they were gone, Jason turned to Sylvia. "Wow, that was exciting. Is selling antiques always this interesting?" he barked out with laughter.

Sylvia frowned, "Jason, that's not nice. This is serious. That man might have murdered Hubert."

Jason plopped onto a stool and spun himself around in a circle. "I don't think so. He reminds me of an old friend. He's the type to steal, bully and boss, but not hurt anyone for real. Especially since he seems to actually care about his mother."

"I better call Bill to come pick me up. He is not going to be happy about this. He made me promise I would stay calm."

As she stood to move to the back room, the sound of the front door opening again halted her. Sylvia reluctantly turned her head.

"Sylvia, what was the police doing here?" Hatty's inquisitive voice made Sylvia cringe.

"They were here to arrest a man they think may have something to do with stealing the Pendecot coins from my desk."

Hatty's mouth gaped open. "But, I thought they already had Doc Holiday?" A sudden thought seemed to occur to Hatty. "But the man who the police had with them, he was in my shop earlier asking if I had any furniture from the Pendecot estate."

"Yes, he admits he stole the coins from my desk and was trying to locate the lost jewels. He thought they might be in another piece of furniture."

Hatty picked up a Dresden China figurine, looked at the price, then set it down again. "No, I don't think those jewels were hidden in furniture. I think they were hidden somewhere in the house."

Jason leaned over. "Why do you think that, Miss Hatty?"

Hatty stared at him but said to Sylvia. "When I was a young girl, I went to a Christmas party at the Pendecot mansion. I remember my father talking to Mary

Pendecot. He said something about how nice her jewels were but how dangerous it was to keep them in the house. I remember she laughed and told him she kept them hidden in a special place in the house, where no one would ever find them."

Sylvia stood silently listening. She didn't want to stop Hatty's words.

"I remember Mary Pendecot smiled at him. Before she walked away, she said, 'Endless reflections, endless reflections.' Then she drifted away from my father."

"What do you think she meant by that?" Jason asked.

Hatty shrugged. "Sylvia, do you think that man killed Hubert? Oh, my! It's terrible to think he was in my shop today, and I was alone with him. That's it. I am going to hire an assistant for sure." Hatty turned and rushed out of the store.

Sylvia took a deep breath and moved to the back room. She called for Bill then sat waiting. She could hardly wait to get home and get in bed.

CHAPTER ELEVEN

Sylvia placed the red and purple hat on her head. She was looking forward to the monthly Red Hat Society meeting. Especially tonight, because it was being held at a small, local Italian restaurant. Most visitors to the area chose to eat seafood, but from time to time Italian was just what the doctor ordered.

Of course, it's all ridiculous, dressing in purple and wearing a red hat, but I wouldn't pass up the opportunity to spend the evening with an amusing group of ladies.

Bill was at her door promptly at six, ready to drive her to the restaurant. As they drove along the gulf, Sylvia wondered what she would do without Bill.

"Bill, why don't you stay at the restaurant and eat, my treat."

"That sounds wonderful. It's one of my favorite places to eat. But, all those women in red hats, running around, I'm not sure."

"Oh, Bill. You can find a nice quiet corner."

Bill glanced up in the rearview mirror. The lines around his eyes crinkled as he smiled.

When they reached the restaurant, Bill parked and escorted Sylvia inside. She drifted into the room filled with women wearing red hats, and Bill waited for a table.

As he waited, a woman stepped up beside him and cleared her throat.

"Excuse me, did I see you come in with Miss Sylvia?"

Bill nodded. He didn't know the woman, but he didn't necessarily know all of Sylvia's acquaintances.

"I'd love to speak with her, but I can see she's busy with the group in there. You see, Miss Sylvia was supposed to contact me the next time she discovered a historic diary in the area. I'm writing a book about the local history."

The word diary made Bill stiffen.

"You don't know if she has located one, do you?"

"No. I'm only the taxi driver."

The woman laughed. "Oh, come now. Everyone knows you and Sylvia are best friends. I'm sure she would confide in you."

Just then the Maître d' stepped up and offered to take Bill to his table.

"I'm sure if Miss Sylvia told you she would contact you, she will... when she has something to show you." Bill huffed as he walked away.

When he looked back, the woman had turned and was glaring across the room at Miss Sylvia. The look on her face made Bill uncomfortable.

An hour later, when Bill took the final bite of his tiramisu, Sylvia appeared next to the table.

She seemed relaxed and happy.

"Bill, did you enjoy your dinner?"

Bill tossed down the napkin and stood. "Yes, Ma'am. It was delicious."

"Oh, I'm so glad. Well, it's official. The ladies have voted me in as president of the group. Of course, that's only because I'm the oldest one in the room."

"You don't act half as old as some of them."

Sylvia nodded. "Did I see you talking to someone earlier? An old friend? She could have joined you."

Bill's eyebrows drew together.

"Not my friend. She said she was a friend of yours. Wanted to know if you'd found any local diaries lately because she was writing a book."

Sylvia looked surprised. "Hmm, well, I have a friend named Eileen who is writing a book about local history. I did promise if I found a diary, I'd let her know. But since I found the Pendecot diary, I haven't had time to contact her. But I don't think that looked like Eileen."

On the drive home, Sylvia nibbled her bottom lip. "I think I'll call Eileen tomorrow. Ask if that was her you met."

"Good idea. If it was, I'm sorry to say I was a bit cold to her. The thought of that diary got my shackles up. I wish you would give it to the police."

"But Bill, I tried. Officer McClan is sure the diary has nothing to do with Hubert's death. He is positive that the whole thing is about those coins. I'll tell you what. I'll finish reading the diary tonight, and tomorrow I'll take it Officer McClan and insist he keep it until Hubert's death is completely solved."

Bill was silent, but inside he wished Miss Sylvia would just get rid of the diary right away.

Sylvia closed the diary, unsatisfied. *Most boring thing I've ever read, but as far as I can see there is no reference to where she may have hidden her jewels, if that's what she did with them at all. The only significant thing I can find is that Mary Pendecot was a bitter woman. She resented Alice's childish interest in the jewels.*

"Today I put my jewels away so that Alice cannot touch them or play with them. She has no interest in me, only the bright shiny jewelry. I wish she loved me as a granddaughter should. Am I really so unlovable?"

Throughout the diary were sketches of different rooms in the Pendecot house, it seemed the woman had hoped to be an artist but was never allowed to indulge her desires so she was content with drawing in her diary.

There was one sketch of the library, one of the dining room, a sketch of the desk Sylvia had purchased and finally a sketch of the wall of small mirrors Sylvia had noticed in the mansion.

Sylvia squinted, searching the drawings, hoping to find some kind of clue; but nothing came to light.

There was one thing that bothered her. It was something about the sketch of the wall of mirrors, but she couldn't put her finger on it.

"Miss Sylvia, customer out here. He's asking about the books. I don't know enough to answer his questions." Jason had poked his head into the back room with a look of desperation on his face.

Sylvia laughed. "Okay, Jason. I'll be right out." Sylvia made her way to the front. However, when she saw the customer standing by the bookshelves, she stopped. It was the short blonde man who had casually looked at the desk at the estate sale.

She hesitated before moving forward but finally glided across the room.

"Jason says you have some questions

about books?" She stopped beside the man. He looked up, slightly startled.

"Oh, yes. I was just wondering about your first editions. Do you have a special section where you keep them?"

Sylvia glared at him suspiciously. "Are you sure it's first editions you want, or is it diaries?"

The man shook his head. "No, I'm a book collector. Not really interested in diaries."

"What about coins? Collect old coins, do you?"

The man seemed confused and murmured, "No, just books."

Sylvia scolded herself. The man was obviously not after the diary or coins. She led him to the first edition bookshelf and left him happily perusing them.

What is wrong with me? she asked herself. *I can't go around assuming everyone who walks in the door is after that stupid diary.*

Later that day, Sylvia sat at Cup N Cake, drinking a cup of coffee. She watched as all the locals came and went. Almost everyone stopped and asked how she was doing or wanted to discuss Hubert's murder.

At one point, the door opened, and her friend Eileen entered the shop. She didn't notice Sylvia but headed straight to the counter and ordered.

Sylvia wanted to speak with her to find out if she was the woman who approached Bill. She assumed once Eileen turned and noticed her, she would come over and talk to her.

Just then, a man entered and moved in line behind Eileen. Her friend turned around and started speaking to him in an animated way. Sylvia sat staring at them, her heart palpitating from the shock. She was surprised. The man was the blonde gentleman who had been looking for books in her shop.

Now Sylvia was suspicious. First, Eileen asking about the diary, and then the man searching her bookshelves. Was it actually a subterfuge? Had he been watching, searching, hoping to find information about the diary? And what could Eileen have to do with it?

Eileen and the man left Cup N Cake together, never even speaking to Sylvia

CHAPTER TWELVE

"Bill, I'm concerned about Eileen." Sylvia explained to Bill as they sat in her parlor sipping a cup of tea. Most taxi drivers wouldn't be invited into a person's house, but Sylvia and Bill had formed such a bond of friendship over the years of Bill driving her everywhere, Sylvia often asked him in for tea.

Bill sipped the tea then set his cup down on the small end table. "Why?"

"Well, first it seems she approached you with questions about a diary, then I see her talking to the man who was in my shop the other day."

Bill cocked his head. "Did he ask about the diary?"

Sylvia sat back with a huff. "That's just it; he didn't. He only wanted to look at my first edition books. At first, I thought he was looking for information on the diary or the coins, but I had finally convinced myself he wasn't interested in the diary."

"But now?"

"Now that I've seen him with Eileen, both so friendly, it has stirred up all my questions again."

Bill reached over and patted his friend's hand in a gentle manner. "Now, Sylvia. Don't get all riled up. There's sure to be some kind of explanation. Why not ring up Eileen on the phone?"

Sylvia set her teacup down. "Do you think I should, really?"

"Yes, really." He assured her. "I'm sure you will find there is something quite innocent in it all."

Sylvia stood and placed the teacups on the tea tray and lifted it to carry it to the kitchen.

Bill stood. "I better get going. You make that call as soon as you can. Call me at six tonight, let me know what you found out."

Sylvia laughed as she walked from the room. "I promise to call you."

Bill slipped on his jacket and walked out

the front door, got in his taxi and drove away.

Sylvia had just finished eating a small casserole. The aroma filled the air.
Mmm, I love New England Shepard Pie. It's always been my favorite.
She was sitting at the table, pen in hand, with the diary opened. She had decided to go through it again, and make notes, to see if she had missed any type of cryptic, hidden message, which would lead to the answer of the missing jewels.

Suddenly, she heard a sound, and her head popped up. Her eyes opened wide.

"What are you doing here? How did you get into my house?"

Her eyes scanned the person and landed on the small gun, pointed straight at her.

"I've come to get that diary. I've tried several times but failed. Now, you've had it long enough to read the whole thing. You must know where the Pendecot jewels are."

Sylvia's lip trembled. "I assure you, I don't."

The person waved the gun slightly. "We are going to the Pendecot mansion. You will show me where the jewels are."

Sylvia shook her head. "I...I really don't know."

Sylvia watched as a crazed expression seemed to cross over the person's face. She swallowed and nodded. "I'll come along with you; perhaps we can figure it out together."

A strange laugh gurgled across the room, making Sylvia cringe. The pen in her hand moved quickly across the paper, then she set it down, picked up the diary and began to walk out of the room.

"I'm positive something has happened to Miss Sylvia." Bill's voice trembled as he spoke into his cell phone. "I'm standing right here in her kitchen. She's not here, but she wrote across her note pad in large letters PENDECOT MANSION."

Officer McClan ran a hand through his hair. He didn't want to rush over if Miss Sylvia had just gone out with some friends. However, he knew as well as anyone else, she never went anywhere unless Bill drove her.

"I'll head over to the Pendecot mansion. You stay there in case she returns." Bill mumbled an answer. He knew Bill would probably beat him to the mansion.

"Now look, I don't want to hurt you. I never wanted to hurt anyone, but you know what I'm capable of so just tell me where the jewels are hidden."

Sylvia's knees felt weak. Her stomach cramped, and she thought she might faint. She held onto the railing on the front porch.

"How will we get in?"

"Oh, you know old people. They always hide a key around. I found it a few days ago."

Sylvia's captor slipped the key in the lock, turned it and opened the door.

"We won't be able to see anything," Sylvia pulled back.

"The electricity hasn't been turned off yet. Probably will be tomorrow. I'll just turn the hall light on."

Sylvia moved toward the door and stepped inside. She realized, if she were younger, she could have made a run for it, gotten away. But at her age, she decided going along was her best chance. She only hoped Bill would miss her and find her hurriedly scratched note.

They were both in the hall. The front door was closed and locked behind them. "Now, show me where the jewels are!"

"I honestly don't know where they are. I read the entire diary, I took notes, I tried to figure it out, but I didn't find any clues."

A hard hand grabbed her wrist and twisted. Sylvia gasped in pain. "Then I suggest you start looking around. See if anything comes to mind. I'm not leaving until I have those jewels, and you're not leaving alive if I don't get them."

Sylvia rubbed her wrist and nodded. "So, you killed Hubert?"

"Yes. That other fool hit him in the head and got to the coins in the desk before I could. But, I still thought the diary was in the desk so when he started to roust around, I killed him."

Sylvia swallowed and stared at the gun pointed at her. *Lord, help me.*

Sylvia began to walk through each room, trying to recall anything in the diary that might give her some indication of where the jewels were hidden, but after a half hour she was no closer to finding them.

Just as she was about to collapse from the fear and excitement, she stepped into the hallway and glanced up at the wall of mirrors. She stood for some time staring at them.

What is it about these mirrors that continue to bother me?

Suddenly, she opened the diary and began to flip through the pages, until she found the page with the sketch of the mirrored wall.

"That's it." She almost shouted.

"What's it?"

"The mirrored wall. There is one mirror, right in the middle that isn't set in as far and is a bit crooked. That mirror is circled in the diary sketch."

The murderer's eyes searched the wall then an evil grin spread across her face.

"So that's where she hid them. I should have known; she was always singing that strange song about endless reflections. She was taunting me with it."

"Alice, may I please sit down?" Sylvia asked the woman. It was obvious she planned to begin ripping the mirror from the wall.

Alice barely acknowledged her with a

curt nod. "Just don't move."

"Why don't you think Mary Pendecot left her money and jewels to you?" Sylvia asked. She hoped Bill had contacted the police by now and would show up soon. If Alice found the jewels behind the mirror, she would probably kill Sylvia and leave her body behind.

"She hated me. She caught me a few times trying on the jewels, and she hid them away. She told me that I was naughty to get into her jewelry box, and now that they were hidden I would never see them again. But I vowed to find them and keep them."

Sylvia sank onto a hard chair against the wall.

"I came to visit her every year. Pretended to love her. I was good to her, but she would never show me the jewels again. I searched this house over and over again, but I could never find them. She also hid her diary somewhere in the desk, but I was never able to get to it."

"And are you the one who broke into my store?"

"Yes. I thought you found the diary and added it to your book collection. Then I thought you had it in your purse..."

Sylvia sat quietly, watching as Alice reached out and touched the mirror. She began to twist, and Sylvia heard the clicking sound.

"It wasn't even locked." Alice cried out in surprise.

The small mirror swung forward, revealing an opening behind it.

"This was clever," Alice started to reach her hand into the opening, but suddenly her wrist was caught, and the gun was yanked from her other hand.

She'd been so busy with the mirrors, she hadn't noticed Bill and Officer McClan enter the room. Officer McClan grabbed the gun, while Bill stopped her from touching the jewels.

Alice turned crazed eyes on the men and screamed, "No, no... you must let me have my jewels. You must..." The woman whimpered.

But Officer McClan placed the handcuffs on her and was already steering her out the door. Over his shoulder, he called out, "Bill, find those jewels, then you and Miss Sylvia come to the station. We are going to need statements from you both."

Bill reached in and pulled out a large velvet bag. He slipped it open and gave a long whistle.

Sylvia pushed herself to a standing position, moved across the room and looked into the bag. She gave her head a shake.

"It's sad to think some pretty rocks could make a woman lose her mind. You know, I really think Alice Pendecot is crazy. But, perhaps, Mary was too. So much of her diary was filled with her strange phobias and fears about people trying to steal her jewels."

"Must run in the bloodline."

"Yes, and Mary hated Alice because Alice loved the jewels and not her."

Bill turned, and Sylvia placed her hand in the crook of his arm. They walked out of the mansion together as comfortable friends.

"Shall I write about all this in my blog?" Sylvia asked Bill.

"Hmm, maybe you should write a book about it. Sounds more like a mystery to me."

"But I wasn't able to solve it. I didn't even suspect Alice until she showed up with a gun. I was sure Eileen and the blonde-haired man were guilty."

Bill laughed. "Well, that's a whole other mystery to solve."

Bill opened the taxi door, and Sylvia slid in. Before he could close the door, she looked up at him and said,

"Bill, there's going to be an estate sale in

New Hampshire a few days before the Coast Drive Mile Long Yard Sale. Gathe, Jennifer and Jason are working it together. Gathe assures me there are rooms full of books and several old desks. I'm sure I'll find a diary there."

Bill groaned and closed the door; but as he walked around to the front, a deep chuckle tumbled out of him.

TERESA IVES LILLY

Teresa Ives Lilly loves to write Christian Fiction. In general, she writes novella length romance, but has been known to write a mystery or two and full-length novels.

Her novel, "Orphan Train Bride" quickly went to number one on Amazon's best seller list and stayed in the top ten for two weeks when first published.

She has participated in many novella collections which have also been on the Amazon's best seller list.

Teresa would love to hear from her readers. Readers can follow Teresa at www.teresalilly.wordpress.com

Teresa is always thankful for positive reviews left on Amazon for her books.

Teresa resides in San Antonio, Texas.

www.ingramcontent.com/pod-product-compliance
Lightning Source LLC
LaVergne TN
LVHW092301280625
814963LV00016B/244